PRAISE FOR TAMMY L. GRACE

"I had planned on an early night but couldn't put this book down until I finished it around 3am. Like her other books, this one features fascinating characters with a plot that mimics real life in the best way. My recommendation: it's time to read every book Tammy L Grace has written."
— *Carolyn, review of Beach Haven*

"*A Season of Hope* is a perfect holiday read! Warm wonderful and gentle tale reflecting small town romance at its best."
— *Jeanie, review of A Season for Hope: A Christmas Novella*

"This book is a clean, simple romance with a background story very similar to the works of Debbie Macomber. If you like Macomber's books you will like this one. The main character, Hope and her son Jake are on a road trip when their car breaks down, thus starts the story. A holiday tale filled with dogs, holiday fun, and the joy of giving will warm your heart."
— *Avid Mystery Reader, review of A Season for Hope: A Christmas Novella*

"This book was just as enchanting as the others. Hardships with the love of a special group of friends. I recommend the series as a must read. I loved every exciting moment. A new author for me. She's fabulous."
—*Maggie!, review of Pieces of Home: A Hometown Harbor Novel (Book 4)*

"Tammy is an amazing author, she reminds me of Debbie Macomber... Delightful, heartwarming...just down to earth."
— *Plee, review of A Promise of Home: A Hometown Harbor Novel (Book 3)*

"This was an entertaining and relaxing novel. Tammy Grace has a simple yet compelling way of drawing the reader into the lives of her characters. It was a pleasure to read a story that didn't rely on theatrical tricks, unrealistic events or steamy sex scenes to fill up the pages. Her characters and plot were strong enough to hold the reader's interest."
—*MrsQ125, review of Finding Home: A Hometown Harbor Novel (Book 1)*

"This is a beautifully written story of loss, grief, forgiveness and healing. I believe anyone could relate to the situations and feelings represented here. This is a read that will stay with you long after you've completed the book."
—*Cassidy Hop, review of Finally Home: A Hometown Harbor Novel (Book 5)*

"Killer Music is a clever and well-crafted whodunit. The vivid and colorful characters shine as the author gradually reveals their hidden secrets—an absorbing page-turning read."
— *Jason Deas, bestselling author of Pushed and Birdsongs*

"I could not put this book down! It was so well written & a

suspenseful read! This is definitely a 5-star story! I'm hoping there will be a sequel!"

—*Colleen, review of Killer Music*

"This is the best book yet by this author. The plot was well crafted with an unanticipated ending. I like to try to leap ahead and see if I can accurately guess the outcome. I was able to predict some of the plot but not the actual details which made reading the last several chapters quite engrossing."

—*0001PW, review of Deadly Connection*

COLD KILLER

A COOPER HARRINGTON DETECTIVE NOVEL

TAMMY L. GRACE

LONE MOUNTAIN PRESS

Cold Killer
A novel by
Tammy L. Grace

www.tammylgrace.com
Facebook: https://www.facebook.com/tammylgrace.books
Twitter: @TammyLGrace

Published in the United States by Lone Mountain Press, Nevada

ISBN 978-1-945591-25-9 (paperback)
ISBN 978-1-945591-24-2 (eBook)
FIRST EDITION
Cover by Elizabeth Mackey Graphic Design
Printed in the United States of America

ALSO BY TAMMY L. GRACE

Remember to subscribe to Tammy's exclusive group of readers for your gift, only available to readers on her mailing list. **Sign up at www. tammylgrace.com. Follow this link to subscribe at https://wp.me/ P9umIy-e** and you'll receive the exclusive interview she did with all the canine characters in her Hometown Harbor Series.

Follow Tammy on Facebook by liking her page. You may also follow Tammy on book retailers or at BookBub by clicking on the follow button.

"Hope is the thing with feathers that perches in the soul – and sings the tunes without the words – and never stops at all."—Emily Dickinson

COLD KILLER
A COOPER HARRINGTON DETECTIVE NOVEL

Book 4

1

Johnny pulled his baseball hat on, adjusted his backpack, and brushed his hand across the bicycle leaning against the rusty and faded Winnebago he'd called home for the last few months. Today, he was on the outskirts of some small town in Georgia, not far from Chattanooga. These last few weeks he'd been all over Mississippi, Alabama, and Georgia but would soon be back home in Tennessee. The life of carnival workers, or carnies, as they were known, wasn't something he enjoyed, and Johnny was glad his time on the road was coming to an end.

Johnny nodded to the young man he had met only hours ago and handed him the keys to the RV. "Take good care of her, Nate."

The skinny kid with dishwater-blonde hair smiled and flicked a cigarette from the box Johnny had given him earlier when he had been sitting outside his old Winnebago. Nate had wandered into the camp, searching for the carnival boss, and came upon Johnny. Nate announced he was looking for work and asked Johnny to point him to the man in charge.

Nate was around Johnny's age and had worked a couple of years as a mechanic, but the nomad life of a carny had drawn him to the field on the edge of town. He was looking for a bit of adventure with his job. The idea sprang to Johnny's mind in a matter of moments as he listened to Nate. He offered him the old RV and all her contents, along with the cigarettes he no longer needed, since he only smoked them to fit in and join in the conversations the workers had when they gathered for their breaks.

"You'll find a few clean work shirts in the closet, and I'll leave you this one." He wrinkled his nose when he sniffed at his armpit. "But you'll need to wash it." Johnny slipped out of the blue shirt he was wearing, with the signature crown patch embroidered with Royal Amusement on the chest pocket. He smoothed the t-shirt he was wearing underneath. "I almost forgot and took off wearing it." He handed it to Nate.

"Remember, wait a couple of hours to give me time to get out of here and then go knock on Rex's trailer. Tell him you're my cousin and that I had to take off, but I vouched for you and gave you my trailer. You'll take my job. You've got way more mechanical experience, and he'll be desperate for the help since I didn't tell him I was leaving, and the carnival starts tomorrow."

Nate grinned and shook Johnny's hand. "I really appreciate it. I can't believe y'all are just giving me this place, plus your bike and everything. It's real good of ya."

Johnny took in his lanky frame, thinking they could pass for brothers, except Nate looked like he could use some hearty meals to put a little meat on his skinny bones. "You're in luck because I just stocked the cupboards, so have something to eat and take a rest while you wait for me to get to town. Don't talk to anyone."

With that, Johnny set out across the back part of the empty field that connected with the road to town. Johnny intended to disappear into the wind, much like when he arrived on the scene. He didn't need anyone to notice him.

As he walked along the road, the low, hot sun beating on his back, his heart felt lighter for the first time since he'd left Nashville months ago. He had the answers and the proof or at least enough to show his dad, who could get to the bottom of it all. He chuckled to himself, remembering how Nate's eyes lit up as if he had hit the lotto when Johnny offered him the RV. To think that old trailer and a low-paying job could bring that much happiness to someone made something deep inside Johnny ache. He had come to have a new respect and appreciation for the carnies. They didn't have much, but they were truly happy and pitched in to help one another. It was an eclectic community, where the liquor sometimes flowed too easily, and hygiene was questionable, but underneath, most of them had kind hearts.

It had taken more than two months for Johnny to figure out what was going on at Royal Amusement Company, but now he finally had the evidence and couldn't wait to show his father. Frank Covington, the owner of the company and his dad, had no idea his son had infiltrated the carnival and posed as a casual laborer in an effort to get to the bottom of the horrible accidents that had taken the lives of five children earlier in the year.

Unlike one of the small traveling carnivals where everyone knew each other and was like a small family, Royal was huge. The division Johnny was with consisted of more than fifty people who moved together from town to town and set up the rides and games. It was hard, dirty work, not something Johnny would enjoy doing for a career, but he was intrigued by the members of the division who loved the life and relished the freedom it offered.

Johnny was relieved nobody gave him a second glance, and Rex, the carnival boss, took no notice of him when Johnny approached him for a job earlier in the summer. Rex was in need of workers and outside of getting Johnny to fill out his name on a line in a notebook, he asked no questions. Along with no forms and no inquiries came the promise of being paid in cash each week, with a small advance for the first week. Without more than a glance and a handshake, Johnny and his old rusted 1976 RV were welcomed into the group of unusual characters who made up Royal's largest division.

It wasn't exactly a warm welcome. The workers who had been together for a long time weren't quick to socialize or partake in small talk with new arrivals. Casual laborers came and went like a muggy breeze in summer, and most of the old timers didn't bother to learn their names. Johnny was assigned to work the bumper cars and had to worm his way into conversations with the operators of the big rides—the dangerous rides. The whole reason he was there.

Along with the tragic loss of five children, and three others severely injured in two different accidents earlier in the year, Johnny had also lost his mother. She had become despondent and depressed after the last incident. The unthinkable tragedies had impacted his father, but they had shattered his mother into a million tiny pieces and no matter what they did, they couldn't put her back together. She took a lethal cocktail of pills and vodka one afternoon and never woke up.

Johnny was heartbroken and couldn't bear the loss of his mother, finding it hard to concentrate on his studies. He had to do something. Joining the carnival, undercover, was the only thing he could think to do. His father spent every waking moment at the office and relegated the care of Johnny's little sister Lindsay to a nanny or the mothers of her school friends. Johnny did his best to attend his classes at Vanderbilt and came home on weekends to try to comfort Lindsay.

When Johnny finished the spring semester at school, he used his generous allowance and the credit card his father paid without question and set off on his summer sleuthing mission. Johnny didn't divulge his plan, fearing his father would object, and only told him he was spending the summer with friends, traveling the country, to which Frank barely nodded his approval, telling his son money was no object.

Johnny hated leaving Lindsay but knew he'd never rest until he got to the bottom of what had gone wrong with the carnival rides that took the lives of those innocent children and robbed him of his mother.

Yesterday, Johnny had ridden his bike down the same road a few miles to the used car lot where he'd taken the cash he had been saving up and bought a used motorcycle. It was one of those car lots where cash was king and when Johnny said he didn't have identification, they didn't blink an eye and filled out the sales forms. Today they were open late, and he would pick it and a helmet up and make his way back to Nashville. He would find a hotel and a real shower along the way.

He'd figure out what to do about the motorcycle paperwork being in his fake name when he got home. He didn't need the hassle of anyone connecting him to his dad or Royal Amusement as he tried to stay under the radar until he was back in Nashville. He finally turned off the road and onto the lot of Abe's Affordable Autos, the sweat trickling down his back and across his forehead.

When he opened the office door, the cool air of the window-mounted swamp cooler greeted him. He ignored the dank and musty smell inside, helped himself to a drink of water from the fountain, and took a chair outside the salesman's office, letting the chilled air waft over his skin. Johnny spotted the payphone right outside the door and toyed with calling his dad again.

He'd rung him yesterday but had to leave a message on his answering machine. He told his dad that he was with the division outside of Rome, Georgia, and had been posing as a carny over the summer using the name of Johnny Green but had uncovered the reason behind the rides failing. He told his dad he had some proof but would need his help to figure it out since everything pointed to the problem being at the corporate office, not in the field. He promised to be home in a day or two. He didn't have time to say more before the machine cut him off.

After several minutes, the salesman with a thick moustache came out of his office, pumping the hand of his newest customer and congratulating him on his smart purchase. He gave Johnny a wink and promised to collect the keys to the motorcycle and get him on his way.

Johnny noticed a vending machine in the corner. A cold cola would hit the spot. He dug into his front pocket for some quarters to pop into the machine and rested the cool can against the back of his neck before popping it open and chugging down almost half of it.

He wandered outside to the payphone and having used his change for the drink, reached into his back pocket and then the other one. Gritting his teeth, he stifled a foul word. He had forgotten his wallet. Of all the things he had to leave behind in the motorhome. He'd have to hurry back and grab it. He had hoped to avoid having anyone, especially Rex, see him leaving, but he couldn't leave his real identification behind.

While Johnny berated himself, the salesman arrived with his keys and told Johnny the bike was ready to roll, pointed to it parked at the entrance, all cleaned up and shiny with a temporary plate and a full tank of gas. Johnny shook his hand in thanks and hurried to climb onto it, downing the rest of his cold drink before he started the engine.

He motored onto the two-lane road, enjoying the breeze, which wasn't cool, but at least dried the sweat from his body.

As he rounded the last bend in the road, he saw a plume of black smoke rising from the carnival site. He slowed the throttle and instead of driving directly down the road, he made his way along an empty field that bordered the land. When he got closer, he gasped.

The breeze carried the acrid smell of smoke, and it filled his nose and coated his throat. Black clouds of it poured from his motorhome, which was a raging inferno, fully engulfed in flames. His pulse pounded in his throat as he weighed his options. "Nate," he whispered, his heart falling, hoping he wasn't in the RV.

His wallet was a lost cause, and there was no point in going back. He didn't need the questions or attention from the local authorities. He turned the bike and headed for the highway that would take him to Chattanooga in a couple of hours.

He was anxious to get home and talk to his dad, but torn between the desire to see his family and the need to know what had happened to his RV. He hadn't even been gone for two hours and couldn't imagine what had transpired at the carnival site. He wanted to find out but wasn't sure how to go about it without drawing attention to himself.

He hadn't eaten much and planned to grab something on the road, but the heat and his lightheadedness made it a priority. He saw a drive-in restaurant sign ahead and pulled off the road and into one of the shaded stalls. He had a bit of emergency cash stashed in his backpack and dug into the inner pocket to retrieve it while he scanned the menu board.

A young woman with blue eyes, rimmed with thick lashes that reminded him of Lindsay's, took his order, and he made his way to the restroom to wash his hands. On his way back, he spotted two sheriff's deputies seated at one of the outdoor tables in front of his stall. His heart beat faster, worried they would ask him for identification or the paperwork for the motorcycle. He took a few deep breaths and tried to calm his nerves as he told himself they had no reason to ask him anything. He looked like a normal guy stopping for some grub while taking his new bike for a spin. He walked by them at a casual pace and heard them mention the fire at the carnival site.

His waitress delivered his food on a tray and since he lacked a window for the tray hangers, she suggested he sit at the small table behind the officers. He thanked her and took a long drink from the orange slush he had ordered. While he dug into his double cheeseburger and fries, he continued to listen to the officers, hoping to pick up on any more tidbits.

The one seated with his back toward Johnny said, "Sarge said they called Doc to the scene. I mean obviously the guy is dead, burnt to a crisp, but they need his official sign off. The fire chief said it looked like he was asleep, and the thing exploded, probably caused by a faulty pilot light on the stove or water heater. You know those old RVs don't have all the safety features like the new ones. It wouldn't take much to fill the inside with propane if the pilot light was out."

The other deputy spoke. "That's a shame. Another drunk carny, I guess. Sarge said they recovered the remains of a wallet, so if it's not too damaged, they should have an identification soon enough."

Johnny's hopes fell, and the burger felt like a heavy brick in his gut. Nate was dead. There had been nothing wrong with the RV. It was old, but he had made sure it was safe. He'd slept in there for the last few months without a problem and never had a propane leak or the pilot light go out. It didn't make sense.

The two deputies didn't have time to say more before they received a call and dashed to their patrol car. Johnny paid his bill and felt awful for leaving a skimpy tip but wanted to conserve his cash. What they said about the wallet at the scene sank in—*they're going to think I'm dead.* Nobody knew Nate was there.

As the miles ticked by, his mind churned with scenarios. If they could identify his wallet, the carnies and Rex would know Johnny Green was a fake. Everyone would know the son of Frank Covington, owner of the largest amusement company in the United States, had been posing as Johnny Green.

What a mess. They'd probably think his dad put him up to spying on them. Nobody knew where he was. Well, nobody that is, except his father.

It was getting dark and with every mile he got closer to Nashville, unease settled over Johnny. He kept driving, unsure of what to do. Could the fire have been deliberate? Did someone find out what he was doing and try to silence him? What if his dad was involved?

2

TWENTY-FIVE YEARS LATER

M yrtle smiled at the two men who without fail, occupied the same booth at Peg's Pancakes every Friday morning. She refilled Coop's coffee cup and set another serving of homemade jam at Ben's plate. Coop added a sprinkle of sugar to his cup. "So, you were saying you need us to look at some cold cases?"

Ben nodded as he slathered his toast with Peg's blackberry jam—almost as famous as the pecan pancakes Coop was eating. "Right, we received some special funding to try to clear some old cases and don't have the manpower, so you were the first one who came to mind. Do you have some time?"

Coop nodded, sopping up a puddle of maple syrup with a wedge of pancake. "We're a bit slow, so that would be great."

Ben grinned as he set down his coffee cup. The mischievous smirk didn't fit the serious nature of his position as chief of detectives for Nashville. "I was hoping you'd say that. I have a whole box of them for you." He cleared his throat and grimaced. "And, uh, we need you to cut us a little deal on your normal hourly rate."

Coop frowned and sat back against the booth, provoking

Ben to chuckle when he read the t-shirt Coop had chosen for the day. IF I AGREED WITH YOU, WE'D BOTH BE WRONG was stenciled across the chest of the long-sleeved green one he wore. Coop glanced down and smirked. "That says it all." He swallowed another sip of the warm liquid he craved and rolled his eyes. "You know I'll do it, so don't pretend you're actually worried."

Ben winked as he shoved his empty plate toward the edge of the table. "Yeah, I know you so well, I already dropped the box off with AB this morning on my way here."

Coop shook his head and laughed. "Betrayed by my oldest friend and the woman who runs my office like a Swiss watch and who I thought had my back."

Myrtle swooped by to collect their plates and drop off the check with a takeout container. "Y'all have a nice day and a great weekend. See ya next Friday."

Ben grabbed the check. "I insist, since you're so agreeable about giving me a discount."

Coop chuckled as he slipped into his jacket. "Quite big of you, really. I mean, after all it is *your* turn to buy."

Ben smirked. "Ah, right. Tell you what, Friday breakfasts will be my treat as long as you're working on a case from my box."

They waved goodbye to Myrtle and stepped onto the sidewalk. Coop clapped Ben on the back. "I'm not too proud to work for food. We'll dig into the box and keep you informed."

On the way to his car, Ben stopped at Coop's Jeep and opened the door to give Gus a few scratches under his chin. "Keep your eye on the big guy," he whispered to him, loud enough for Coop to hear.

Coop drove the few blocks to Harrington and Associates, parked behind the house turned offices, next to AB's green VW Bug, the bright color reminding Coop of a grasshopper and the promise of spring in a few months. The dreary, overcast winter sky matched Coop's Friday mood, but Gus, who never had a bad day, bounded to the back door. Coop turned the knob and followed Gus inside, where they found AB in Coop's office, digging into the file box Ben had delivered.

"Morning, AB," Coop said. "I left you pumpkin pecan pancakes on your desk. Also, Ben promises to buy us breakfast as long as we're working..." He glanced at the piles of folders on the table. "On any of these cases."

"Ooh, we might want to drag it out then?" She wiggled her eyebrows at him. "I was just getting things organized. Cold is an understatement. These cases came right out of the frozen section."

Coop sat down to look while AB went to eat her breakfast. His nose in the air with the possibility of pancakes in his future, Gus followed at her heels. Coop shifted through several files, reading the summary case notes, separating them into stacks he thought of as yes, no, and maybe.

Most of the unsolved cases were around twenty years old, some even older. There were only ten cases in the box, although some of the files were voluminous. Coop scanned all the case sheets, hoping to see his uncle's name on one of them. His excitement fizzled when none of them bore the name of Uncle John as the detective in charge of the case.

He whittled it down to three possible cases he was willing to look into, remembering the reduced fee agreement. Coop made sure Ben understood their current clients came first, and he and AB would work on his cases only when they had free time. He couldn't support the office on the reduced rate and deemed it filler work for slow days. As it was, Ross and Madison were taking days off or doing some side jobs while they waited for the slump that always seemed to follow the holidays to end.

When AB returned to check on his progress, he shoved a stack of files toward her. "Take a look at these three, and you pick the first and maybe only case we'll tackle. These are going to take quite a bit of time." While she gave the files an in-depth review, he went to the kitchen and poured himself a cup of decaf coffee, having already spent his doctor-advised allotment on the real stuff at Peg's, and nibbled on a few of the peanut M&Ms he allowed himself each Friday.

Before AB had a chance to make much progress on the files, Gus' ears perked, and he rushed to the reception area before the sound of the bell on the front door announced a visitor. A lanky man stepped inside, bringing a gust of cold January air with him. He smiled at Gus and stepped to AB's desk.

She came from around the corner and glanced at Gus. "I see you've met our greeter."

The man chuckled as he bent to ruffle the top of Gus' head. "That's the perfect job for such a happy guy." He extended his hand toward her. "I'm Jo, uh, sorry, Dax Covington, and I need to retain Mr. Harrington's services."

AB stepped to her desk and grabbed an intake form. "I'll just gather your basic information, and then we'll get him to meet with you." She smiled and added, "Feel free to call him Coop, everyone does." She made quick work of filling out the form, and Coop came from the kitchen, holding his coffee and one of Aunt Camille's chocolate chunk pecan cookies.

AB raised her eyes. "Coop, Mr. Covington is a new client and would like to speak with you about a legal matter and an investigation."

As AB made the introduction, Coop took in the tall man with his piercing, but tired blue eyes. The wrinkled clothes and bit of scruff that made for a heavy five o'clock shadow accentu-ated Coop's first impression that his new client was weary or worried, or both. Coop gestured to Dax to follow him to his office, with Gus at his heels. Dax took a chair in front of Coop's desk, while Gus hopped onto the leather chair in the corner he had long ago claimed as his.

Moments later, AB returned with a plate of cookies and an offer of hot tea or coffee for Dax. He chose the tea, and Coop's eyes followed the departure of the cup of real coffee AB took with her as she clicked the door shut. Everyone told him it was impossible to tell the difference between decaffeinated and regular coffee by the aroma, but his nose was sensitive, and the steam coming from his cup didn't compare to the rich scent of the cup AB would be enjoying.

Coop gave the form AB had filled out a cursory glance and turned his attention to Dax. "How can we help you?"

Dax sighed. "First, I just got off a plane, dumped my bag at a motel, and have been traveling for the better part of a day, so I apologize for my rather shabby appearance. I'm here because... well, it's a long story that started twenty-five years ago." Coop's forehead creased as he tried to place Dax's accent, which sometimes sounded British. He stifled a chuckle as he glanced at the box of cold cases on his conference table. It must be the day for cold cases.

Dax took a sip from his cup. "Bottom line, I died twenty-five years ago. I need you to help me prove I'm alive and find out who tried to kill me. The bad news is...I think it could have been my dad."

3

Coop stopped his intended sip of decaf. That was a new one for him, though with years of practice, he didn't let on that he was intrigued. He urged Dax to continue and tell him what had happened all those years ago.

Dax recapped the story of the accidents and deaths, along with his mother's suicide and his amateur undercover work, pointing out that he chose to infiltrate the largest division at Royal rather than one of the smaller divisions that had been involved in the accidents. He didn't want to draw attention and was worried he'd be more noticeable in a smaller group.

Dax took a deep breath. "That first night, after the fire, I decided to hole up in a dive motel and get some sleep until I could figure out what to do. I didn't want to go anywhere that I might be recognized."

Coop nodded. "Understandable, and I remember the accidents with the carnival company. I was in college at the time, probably close to your age. That's a lot to handle." He tapped his pen on his notepad and asked Dax the name of the motel and scribbled it down.

Dax reached for his tea. "The next morning, I found a newspaper and read the article about my tragic death and the fact that my dad was surprised to discover I was impersonating a carnival worker. There was a companion article about my dad and how brokenhearted he was, having lost my mom earlier in the year and just ready to announce his engagement to Adele, his long-time secretary at the company."

Coop's brows rose. "Was the engagement a surprise to you?"

Dax bobbed his head. "A real punch to the gut. I couldn't believe it, and it made me question everything. Mom hadn't been gone that long, so maybe there was more to her suicide than just being depressed and upset about the accidents. I didn't know what to do and had nobody to ask. I was sick that Nate, the young kid who I gave my RV to, had perished in the fire."

Gus stretched out and off his chair and sat next to Dax, leaning against his leg. Coop smiled at the golden dog, who no doubt sensed Dax's emotions and thought he could use the support.

"I waited until the day of my funeral and snuck back into our house. Mom kept a stash of cash Dad never knew about. She told me it was smart for a woman to always have her own money. She hid it in a purse in her closet. I found it and took that, plus a few clothes and things from my closet, making sure I didn't take much or anything they would notice." He pointed at the expensive watch on his wrist. Coop recognized the iconic stainless-steel band and the sapphire-blue face of the handsome piece.

"This had been a graduation gift that I hid in my closet before I joined the carnival. It would have drawn attention had I worn it when working, but I wanted to take it with me, so I had something to remember Mom by." His eyes glistened, and his voice cracked. "I hated leaving Lindsay most of all."

Coop leaned back in his chair. "I can imagine. I'm sorry you had to go through all that alone." He added another note to his pad and then glanced up at Dax. "Did you know Nate's last name or anything about him?"

He shook his head. "Just that he said he had been a mechanic. I guessed he was close to my age." Dax shrugged. "I was scared and didn't want to be anywhere close to Royal Amusement or Dad. I bought a fake passport and a ticket to Heathrow and disappeared. I've been living in England ever since."

"What brought you back home now?" Coop reached for another cookie and urged Dax to take one.

He smiled and selected one. "I keep up with the paper and noticed an article last week featuring my dad. He donated the funding for a new wing at Vanderbilt Children's Hospital, naming it in my honor. The article talked about how my death had almost destroyed him, and he was so happy to dedicate this project to me, likely his last project, as he has terminal cancer."

Dax hung his head and sighed. "I just have to know. I can't let him die without knowing what really happened. I also haven't exactly been living the high life. I work in a small pub in Cornwall, where I get room and board and have survived on the meager wages and tips I get. It's a beautiful area, and I do well during tourist season, but it also hit me that I'm entitled to part of Dad's estate. I'm tired of being on the run and want to reconnect with Lindsay. I just want my family back…"

It wasn't lost on Coop that Dax couldn't continue and masked it with a long swallow from his mug. Coop reached behind him for a box of tissues and slid it across the desk. "I sympathize and agree if you are Frank's son, you're entitled to your share of the estate. First thing's first, your father and sister are convinced you've been dead for the last twenty-five years, so I think a DNA test is in order to remove any doubt about who you say you are. Agreed?"

Dax nodded. "Yes, I figured that would need to be done. I think it might be easier to approach Lindsay first, especially with Dad being ill."

"What name have you been living under while you've been in England?"

Dax pulled out his passport and handed it to Coop. "John Williams. It was easier to stick with John since I was used to it. Less chance to slip up."

Coop jotted more notes on his legal pad and wrote down the motel where Dax was staying. Coop recognized it as being budget friendly and only a few blocks from Vanderbilt University. "Let me dig into all this a little, and then I'll have AB contact you when we know more and can set up something for next week. In the meantime, we'll take a cheek swab from you and get it to our lab. Does that sound reasonable?"

Dax blew out a breath and smiled. "Yes, that works. I've never told another living soul this story. For the first time in twenty-five years, I feel like a heavy weight has been lifted, and I have someone on my side."

Dax removed a worn and yellowed folder from his leather satchel and handed it to Coop. "These are my notes and what I found related to the accidents. You can go through them and maybe make copies to make sure we keep them safe. I've been protecting them all these years."

Coop hit a button on his phone and summoned AB to handle the copying task. "She'll make us our copies, and we'll give you these back. I'll make sure we keep a set in our safe, just in case. AB and I went to law school together, and she's also a lawyer, although not practicing. So, feel free to tell her anything you would tell me. We approach our cases as partners, and you can trust her with any information."

Coop offered him another cookie and handed him his card with his cell number on it. "We'll be in touch next week. Give me a call if you need anything before that."

Dax smiled as he shook Coop's hand. "Thank you. I've read about you in the papers, too. You've solved some pretty interesting cases, and I like that you're a lawyer, and your uncle was a police detective. It doesn't hurt that you went to Vanderbilt. I had intended to go back there and graduate." His voice trailed off as he said the last words.

Coop put a hand on his shoulder. "Let's see what we can do to help you get your life back."

As soon as AB had Dax on his way, Coop checked his watch, amazed that it was almost closing time. "I'll take Dax's file home, since the chance of me having some extra time in the middle of the night is high." He gave her a quick summary and asked AB to prioritize the research into Dax's past for next week, including the carnival accidents. "Aunt Camille expects us for supper tonight, so we need to get moving."

AB nodded. "Right. I'll be right behind you. I just need to answer a few emails."

Coop and Gus bundled into the Jeep and headed home, taking note that the wintery days of late January were getting a bit longer in that there was still a hint of light on his way home.

With Coop's dad still in town, Camille was in her element. Although Uncle John had been gone for several years, she never got over the loss of his companionship. With Charlie in the house, she had a new purpose and with him recuperating, she doted on him constantly.

He was making great progress with his physical therapy and looked happier than he had in years. The hearty meals, social interaction, and spending time with Coop had done wonders for his spirits. As soon as Coop opened the door, Gus followed his nose to the beckoning smells coming from the kitchen, and Coop lugged the files to his home office in his wing of the house.

The tuxedo hanging on the door of his closet made him grimace. The gala for Aunt Camille's club was tomorrow night.

He toyed with the idea of dropping by the hospital and licking doorknobs with the hope of contracting an illness that would keep him home, but he realized it was probably too late for that. He should have done it a few days ago.

The doorbell chimed, prompting him to hurry to the main part of the house. He found the entryway empty but heard AB's laugh from the kitchen. He discovered her helping Aunt Camille strain pasta and his dad watching from his seat at the granite-topped island counter. "Smells wonderful, Aunt Camille," said Coop, putting his arm around his dad's shoulders.

"Charlie requested spaghetti tonight, so that's what we're having." Camille opened the oven door, and the mouthwatering scent of garlic and butter drifted from it.

Gus lifted his nose higher in the air while Coop reached in and retrieved the foil-wrapped loaves of bread. Camille directed them and within minutes, everything was on the table, Charlie was seated, and she was pouring sweet tea in the glasses at each plate. At Charlie's request, she had cut back on the amount of sugar she normally added, and everyone had adjusted to the new recipe she'd christened as Charlie's tea.

Coop dug into his salad and glanced over at Camille and his dad. "What did you two do today?"

Camille chattered on about their trip to the community center, where Charlie stayed while she had her hair done. "Then we picked up your tuxedos." She winked at Coop. "I left it on your closet door."

AB hid a grin behind her napkin. "I've got my dress ready. It's going to be such a fun event. A few years ago, I went to a wedding out at Lakeview, and it's such a pretty venue. I can't wait to see what it looks like tomorrow night."

Camille beamed with pride. "I chaired the committee and worked with them to choose all the décor elements. It's quite sophisticated and elegant, I think."

Coop raised his brows at AB. "Just don't get so caught up in the ambience, you forget to bid on me." He turned toward his aunt. "This would be so much easier if I could just write you a check and skip the whole thing."

"Oh, it will be a hoot," said Camille. "You hardly ever get dressed up. It'll do you good."

He nodded slowly. "Yeah, that's how I've designed my life. I don't like getting dressed up."

Charlie chuckled and held up his hands. "Surrender is your best option, son. I'm not one for fancy affairs, but your aunt is so excited and..." He smiled across the table at her. "Quite convincing."

"More like a gifted blackmailer," Coop muttered, reaching for another slice of garlic bread.

As they passed serving bowls around the table, Camille glanced at her nephew. "So, are you still a bit slow at the office, Coop? Did you get any new cases this week?"

"As a matter of fact, Ben dumped some cold cases on us this morning. Then a real-live cold case walked through the door. A local man who died twenty-five years ago needs us to prove he's alive and find out who killed him."

Her penciled-on eyebrows rose, and her lips formed a circle. "Ooooh, that sounds so exciting. Who was he? I wish your uncle was still here. He'd probably remember it. He had such a knack for keeping track of all those old cases."

"We haven't gotten very far yet, but he claims to be a Covington. AB is going to dig into some of the old case files and newspaper articles from that time, and we'll get started on it next week. He just came in this afternoon. We still need to verify several things."

Charlie reached for another slice of bread from the platter. "That sounds like an intriguing case. So, a different man died, but everyone believes this guy was dead?"

AB nodded. "Especially because the man thinks his father

may have been the one who killed him. Well, not him, but you know what I mean."

Aunt Camille's forehead creased. "It must be Frank Covington's son Dax? I see his sister at Bella's Salon. We're on the same mani-pedi schedule. She's a lovely woman, as was her mother Laura Beth."

Coop's eyes met hers. "It's confidential, so you can't say a word about it. Not even a hint."

She nodded. "I know how to keep quiet about a case, Coop. Trust me, I did it for years with your uncle." She pushed the platter of bread toward Charlie. "Well, if I know you two, you'll get to the bottom of it in no time." Camille looked around the table. "Who's ready for some ice cream?"

After dessert and a bit more visiting, Coop helped AB into her coat and walked her to the driveway. He retrieved a check from his pocket, made out to the charity with the amount left blank. "Just remember our deal, AB. Money is no object tomorrow night. Whatever it takes, you make sure you win the bid for me."

"I've never seen you so nervous before." She laughed, as she slipped the check into her purse and slid behind the wheel. "You've taken down murderers and stared into the eyes of cold-blooded criminals, yet an evening on a stage with a few women ogling you has you scared out of your wits. You surprise me."

"Remember, I'm trusting you, AB."

With a bit of mischief in her eyes, she smiled and waved as she put the car in gear. He watched her taillights disappear, hoping she was just messing with him.

4

Monday morning, Gus and Coop arrived at the office early. After pushing the button on the coffee maker, he made his way down the hall to his office and got a fire going in the old fireplace. The homey scent of the wood burning and the leather furnishings reminded Coop of Uncle John. The days he spent as a young man, huddled in this office with his beloved and wickedly smart uncle, were some of his favorite memories.

He hadn't gotten much work done over the weekend, not with the whole bachelor auction fiasco. He hated to admit it, but the evening had been fun, filled with laughter and excellent food. More than anything, he had enjoyed seeing his dad so happy. He and Aunt Camille even got on the dance floor. Not that Charlie was able to do much dancing, but they had swayed to an oldies tune they both loved.

AB had come through and won the bid for Coop, at a whopping fifteen hundred dollars, but he wouldn't quibble about the money. At least AB had drawn the prize of a dinner from Houston's, a new and popular venue famous for their steaks, barbecue, and line dancing. They both deserved something nice for their trouble, and a night out there wasn't cheap—not fifteen hundred dollars, but he'd at least get a good meal out of it.

Coop read over the notes he had taken from Friday's meeting with Dax. His gut told him Dax was telling the truth. There was something sincere about his emotions, but Coop liked to follow the trust but verify doctrine and fired up his computer to do some online research into the events of twenty-five years ago.

He found Dax's obituary and marked a few articles about the carnival accidents. Next, he checked the recent coverage of Frank Covington and his donation to Vanderbilt. Instead of his son, Dax could be an imposter who saw the article and thought to take advantage of a rich, dying man.

He started the search into Lindsay Covington, unmarried and living in Nashville. He wanted to dig into the fire and Dax's death in Georgia, but that would take some doing. AB could tackle that when she got into the office. As Coop made a note, Gus took off in a flash of fur. Moments later, AB's voice, that high, sweet one she used just for Gus, drifted through the office.

As was their habit, within thirty minutes, AB came through Coop's office door with a cup of decaf for him and a mug of whatever she was drinking—today the scent of a spicy cinnamon tea drifted from her cup. She sat at the conference table across from him. "Well, did you spend all weekend researching Dax?"

"For a change, no. I didn't work. We had a pretty lazy week-end, hanging out and playing cards most of yesterday." He slid his notepad across the table.

"Having your dad around is good for you." She winked. "Okay, I'll start on the carnival accidents and the fire in Georgia."

"Maybe you can give a ring across the pond to the pub in Cornwall and verify that part of Dax's story. See what they can tell you about John Williams. Our first step is a DNA test with his sister, but I want to be as sure as I can be that Dax is who he says he is. The last thing I want to do is give her false hope or subject her to a fraud."

AB took another swallow from her cup. "That's a tough call, but Dax didn't show any signs he was lying. Over the years, we've developed some pretty good BS meters, and he didn't set off any alarm bells for me."

Coop nodded. "Me either. I just want to get a little background and then figure out the best approach to getting her DNA for a test. Family stuff is always so messy."

"I'll get on it right away. The lab can turn it around in twenty-four hours if Dax wants to pay the premium fee."

"I'll ask him when we get there. I don't think he's got an unlimited budget. I noticed him flinch a bit at the retainer amount he gave us."

Coop added the names of the parents who had lost their children in the carnival accidents to his new fancy whiteboard, which was no longer white. He had treated himself and splurged at the end of the year on a modern glass board that could be controlled from his computer or smart phone and when not in use or when he wanted to cover the contents, he could fill the screen with an image. His old whiteboard had gotten to the point where images had ghosted and left a faint outline, no matter how hard he tried to clean it. This sleek, modern glass one had the advantage of being able to be written on with any type of marker and didn't leave any ghost images. He especially liked that he could put an inviting image on the screen, and nobody would see his lists and notes, which were often messy.

As he added the name of the parents to the list, he didn't want to think they were involved but knew it wasn't out of the realm of possibilities that they would be out for revenge. He'd seen it before where grieving parents decided the people responsible for their loss had to suffer.

AB took her tea and her working file and left Coop to his research and Gus to his nap.

It was well after lunchtime when they gathered in the kitchen for leftover roast beef sandwiches and fresh cookies courtesy of Aunt Camille's kitchen escapades over the weekend and chatted about what they had learned.

AB consulted her notepad. "Richard, the owner of Golden Feather Inn in Cornwall, has nothing but good things to say about John Williams. Confirms he's been in Cornwall for the last twenty-five years, having worked first for Richard's father, and then stayed on when he took over the business about ten years ago. Model employee who worked up to manager, never caused any trouble, said he left to go back to the States and deal with some family estate issues. Richard said John is welcome back if he returns to Cornwall."

Coop nodded as he bit into his sandwich. After taking a drink of iced tea, he referred to his notes. "I found his photo at Vanderbilt and in his obituary and although much older, the Dax we saw Friday matches the younger version."

AB patted the file folder next to her. "Everything he told us checks out. Not to say he couldn't have researched it all, but the timing and facts are solid. I've been reading the evidence he collected. It looks like the workers were falsifying the maintenance reports and replacement of worn parts on the carnival rides. Notes point to corporate being behind the phony records scheme. Trying to save money and stretch out the maintenance intervals. No names were mentioned, always just a reference to corporate putting the pressure on them with bonuses and pay tied to cutting expenses and increasing revenue. Rex, the carnival boss, kept a little note-book, and that's where Dax discovered most of the information."

Coop finished his last bite. "We'll need to get a look at the corporate records and see how the company was structured and who was in leadership positions."

"Right, I'll get on that tomorrow."

As he headed back to his office, Coop tossed the plastic wrap from his sandwich and helped himself to one more cookie. "Since we aren't sure if Dax is Dax, I think it may be wise for us to obtain Lindsay's DNA without asking. I'm not sure I want to put her or Dax through a meeting quite yet and would like to know for sure before we take that step."

"I think we can be reasonably sure she wasn't involved in whatever happened in Georgia. Frank, on the other hand, is another story. He was announcing his engagement with his poor wife dead only six months. That seems fast to me."

Coop raised his brows as he bit into the cookie. "I think Dax had good reason to doubt him." He finished the cookie and asked, "Are you up for a bit of undercover work with Aunt Camille?"

She grinned. "Oh, boy. Aunt Camille is going to be beyond excited. You might be creating a monster."

Coop laughed. "Believe me, I know I am."

With the tidbit Aunt Camille shared about Lindsay's standing appointments at Bella's Salon, Coop put his plan into action on Wednesday. Aunt Camille didn't have much to do, other than engage Lindsay in conversation and keep her occupied, while AB did the heavy lifting.

AB had taken yesterday afternoon off to get acclimated at Bella's Salon in her latest undercover role. She didn't want today to be her first day there, hoping to diminish any attention she might get as a new salon assistant.

Coop could spot AB anywhere, having known her for so long, but when she walked through the door on Wednesday morning, he grinned at the woman standing before him, totally transformed. She wore a curly dark wig laced with gray, dressed in the signature pink scrub-like uniforms everyone wore at Bella's. She had further transformed herself by wearing glasses with a slight tint that masked her blue-green eyes. Sturdy, grandma-looking shoes had replaced the stylish clogs she favored.

Coop couldn't stop staring at her face, which looked like it had aged twenty years. Her skin appeared wrinkled, and her hands had several dark age spots he never remembered. "Wow. You're stunning, but not in a good way. I can't believe how old you look."

She took off her glasses and rolled her eyes. "Your compliments need a bit of work. Might explain why you're single." She laughed. "I have a friend who is a makeup artist, and she helped me with my transformation. Nobody gives older women a second glance, and yesterday proved that point. Not much more than a hello and thank you from a few customers."

"I wish I could go and watch, but I'd stick out like a sore thumb, and I'll eventually have to have a meeting with Lindsay, so would rather she not know about our subterfuge."

AB fixed herself a cup of tea while they chatted. "I know. I feel guilty tricking her but agree we need to know for sure that Dax is her brother before we bring her into the conversation. If he is and we have to come clean, we'll just beg forgiveness and say we were trying to protect her from anyone who would want to take advantage of her."

Despite AB wagging her finger at him, Coop poured himself a cup of real coffee. "Aunt Camille has a ten o'clock appointment too and is bringing some of her cookies to share. Between that and the samples you can collect from her pedicure along with the complimentary facial I arranged with Bella, I think we should have enough material. Just make sure you get the skin and nail trimmings into the plastic bags as soon as possible, so there's no chance of a mix-up."

She nodded and rinsed her empty cup. "I've got it. I'm going to head over there now, so I'm in the groove by the time Lindsay arrives. Once I have her samples, I'll call you and meet you in the alley."

"I'll treat you to a late lunch when we're done today." He chuckled and pointed at her nametag. "That is, after you take all that off and become AB again, Trudy."

"That's the toughest part, remembering to answer to Trudy." She gave Gus a quick pat on the head and collected her purse. "I need to get a move on. I'm parking a few blocks away and walking slower, getting into character, just so there's no chance of anyone connecting me to my new persona."

Gus cocked his head at her, before giving her hand a quick lick as she went out the door. Coop stroked the top of his head. "Don't worry, boy. It's still our AB under all that mess."

To curb his urge to worry about Aunt Camille and AB and their undercover operation, Coop kept busy with some files for one of their corporate accounts and then moved on to study the history of Royal Amusement and Frank Covington. Royal Amusement had sold shortly after Dax's death, and Frank started a new venture in the insurance business. He had built a substantial corporation and had acquired several smaller insurance companies over the years. If Dax was his son, he would be inheriting a fortune.

Coop checked his watch, and it was almost noon with no word yet from AB. Coop put in a call to Ben and asked him for help in getting the old file on the fire at the carnival in Georgia. He'd have more luck getting information out of the authorities than Coop and could do it quicker.

Ben promised to do his best and call Coop the minute he had anything. Coop was just about to dig into Ben's box of cold cases when his cell phone chimed with a text. He let out a long sigh, locked the front door, and motioned to Gus. "Let's go, Gus. AB has our samples."

They made the short drive and swung into the alley that ran behind the strip mall where Bella's Salon was housed. AB was waiting and handed him a large paper bag. She winked when he took it from her. "It worked like a charm. Lindsay should be out of here by one o'clock, and then I'll take my break and disappear, letting Bella know it just isn't working out."

"Great, I'll meet you at The Pickle Barrel around two o'clock. Does that give you enough time to convert yourself?"

She grinned. "Plenty. I'll meet you there and give you a full report." She waved and went back inside the building.

Coop drove to the lab facility he always used. He had called ahead, and they were expecting his samples. He was trying to keep the costs down for Dax and was able to persuade Janice, the lab manager, who AB was convinced had a crush on him, to expedite the test and results at no additional fee. They had already processed Dax's sample from last week and would run it against Lindsay's, looking for a sibling match.

Janice promised to rush it and have the results emailed to him in the morning. She reminded him that sibling tests were more accurate if a parent sample was also obtained. Coop understood that but wasn't in a position to provide any further samples at the moment. He was sure if Dax could be an heir to the Covington fortune, Frank would have no problem providing a sample and paying for a legal test.

He escaped from Janice and her fluttering eyelashes and toothy smile and hurried back to the Jeep. He'd have to take a ribbing from AB about her, but it was worth it to get the quick turnaround and be able to move forward with the next part of the investigation.

He drove back to the office and put in a call to Dax, arranging a meeting with him for tomorrow afternoon, when Coop would know whether he was telling the truth or if he was an opportunistic shyster. Over the years, he'd learned to trust his gut and it was telling him Dax was the real deal. It was also telling him he needed one of the Pickle Barrel's famous brisket sandwiches.

5

Aunt Camille insisted AB join them for supper after their joint performance at Bella's. Coop answered the doorbell and led AB into the dining room where Mrs. Henderson was just putting the last serving bowl on the table. Aunt Camille beckoned them to gather around the table for the wonderful meal, perfect for a chilly winter evening.

As they passed platters of juicy roasted chicken and vegetables and poured rich gravy over perfectly mashed potatoes, Aunt Camille regaled them with her undercover experience at Bella's.

"It was so excitin', and AB was the best. I would have never recognized her. In fact, it took me a few minutes to realize it was her, and I knew the plan." She chuckled, giddy with excitement. "I had no trouble keeping Lindsay distracted. It wasn't out of the ordinary, since we're always quite chatty when we're in the pedicure chairs. The only difference was the plate of cookies I brought to share."

She took a sip of sweet tea and continued, "Like a pro, AB accidentally knocked Lindsay's half-eaten cookie off the edge of the table. She apologized, and I made sure to pass her a new one, while AB slipped the partially eaten one along with the napkin Lindsay had used into her hand. AB was busy cleaning and disposing of things, wearing those latex gloves, so it all just seemed natural. Nobody blinked an eye."

AB nodded. "Yes, it went quite well. Like I predicted, nobody paid me any attention. Collecting the clippings and skin from the pedicure treatment was easy since the technicians use so many clean towels, and I just whisked Lindsay's into the back room and put it in a bag. Same with the facial cotton and washcloths. All the used items are deposited on a clean towel for disposal, which makes collecting them a breeze." She glanced at Coop and raised her brows. "I think our plan was a success and hopefully, we have enough samples for the lab to get a definitive answer."

He finished off the buttery roll he had popped into his mouth. "Janice promised she would email the results in the morning. I think she would have called if the samples weren't adequate."

AB batted her lashes. "Janice would never pass up an opportunity to call you."

Camille's eyes widened. "Do I know Janice?"

Coop shook his head. "No, Aunt Camille. And don't get any crazy ideas. She works at the lab we use, that's all."

Charlie snickered, and AB laughed. "She has a tiny crush on our boy, but sometimes it works to our advantage. Like today. She's rushing the results for us so Coop can meet with Dax tomorrow."

Camille grinned and dug her fork into the potatoes. "I'm just thrilled we pulled it off. Detective work is so excitin'." She stopped mid-bite and glanced at AB. "The technicians told Bella they thought you were the best assistant she'd ever had in the salon. Went on about how attentive you were about keeping the stations neat and clean."

With her head tossed back, AB chuckled. "They're going to

be sad tomorrow when she tells them I decided it wasn't a good fit for me."

Charlie brought his napkin to his lips. "You three have so much fun. I'm going to miss all this excitement when I go back home."

"You could always move here," said Camille, with a sparkle in her pale blue eyes. "We'd love to have you."

Charlie smiled and waved his hand in the air. "Ah, no, I love where I live. It's home and always will be, but I do plan to visit more often. I just hate flying so much."

"Maybe we could talk you into staying for a few months when you come. That way, you'll only have to fly once a year," said Coop, reaching for the gravy. "Or I could drive out and pick you up."

Charlie's grin widened. "I'd love that. There's nothing better than a road trip."

"If it's only one trip a year, I could easily charter a private plane like I did to get you here this time, Charlie," said Camille. "It would be my pleasure to do that for you."

Charlie shook his head. "I've taken advantage of your kindness and hospitality enough. I couldn't let you do that. It's much too expensive."

Camille wagged her finger across the table. "Listen here, Charlie. I've learned you must enjoy life and make the most of every precious moment. Money is meant to be enjoyed and spent. Having you here for company and visiting is worth more than a vault full of gold bars. I would never force you to fly, but that option is always available to you."

Coop eyed his dad. "A wise man once told me it's smarter to surrender."

With that, all four of them erupted into laughter, and Camille retrieved the still-warm peach cobbler.

~

Thursday morning, Coop was at the office early. Sleep had been elusive last night, and he spent most of it looking through old newspaper articles and anything else he could find on Frank Covington—both his personal and business life.

The quick sale of the company after Dax's death drew his attention. Coop ran a bright yellow highlighter over the date and information. It could be a natural reaction to wanting to get rid of the memories surrounding his son's death or it could be something more sinister.

It was still dark outside and too early to call Ben. Coop was antsy to get the file on the fire and investigation into Dax's death. He'd also like to find Nate's family, if Dax's story was true. His family deserved to know what happened to him.

While waiting for Janice's email, Coop dug into the research on Royal Amusement. Frank had started the company almost fifty years ago. First, it had been small and regional and then grew to a nationwide enterprise. With that growth, the management of the company also expanded, but the corporation had been privately held, as was his new corporation.

In checking old records, he noticed the name of Huck Grover who served as the chief financial officer for years. Then, twenty-five years ago, his name disappeared from all the corporate filings for Royal or the new company. Did Huck leave the company and decide not to join Frank in the new venture, or did he get fired?

Coop tapped the keyboard and searched Huck's information. He was now living in Brentwood, just twenty minutes away from Coop's office. He was a few years younger than Frank and had retired from one of the biggest corporations in Tennessee, a shipping company with its headquarters in Memphis. From what Coop gleaned, Huck had left Royal and Nashville and moved to Memphis twenty-five years ago. He'd been living in Brentwood since his retirement almost ten years ago.

Coop scribbled Huck's address and phone number on a legal pad. He checked the time, wandered into the kitchen, and finished off the rest of the pot of coffee he had brewed. He didn't want AB to know he cheated on his daily mug, but without much sleep last night, he craved the jolt of caffeine. He set about loading the filter with decaf and poked the button to brew it.

He also took a cookie from the plate on the counter. He'd been up so long, he was already craving lunch. He had just finished the last bite of cookie when Gus took off for the rear entrance, letting Coop know AB was in the parking lot. He swept the crumbs off his desk and refreshed his email once more.

He was about to groan with impatience, when a new email appeared at the top of the list. It was from Janice and attached to her message was the lab report on the comparison of Lindsay's and Dax's DNA samples. He clicked on his mouse and opened the report. It contained all the scientific data, analysis, and graphs and a short narrative conclusion. Coop smiled as he read it. The two samples showed a high probability of a full sibling match. It wasn't legal or above the threshold for certainty, but it was enough for Coop to invite Lindsay to a meeting and hopefully persuade her to set up a legal test with Frank.

The sound of AB talking to Gus and her footfalls, along with the click of his toenails across the wooden floor, echoed throughout the office. It would be a few minutes before she would appear with a mug of decaf for him and whatever she fancied in her own mug.

Right on cue, she and Gus came through the door, and she handed Coop his coffee, eyeing the oversized cup on his desk that he favored, printed with THEY TOLD ME TO CUT BACK TO ONE CUP PER DAY. He was certain she saw the trace of fresh coffee in the bottom of it and may have guessed that he had filled it twice this morning, but she didn't say anything. He smiled at her. "Great news. Janice just emailed and while not totally conclusive, there's a high chance Lindsay and Dax are siblings. We'll need to get her in and have her meet Dax." AB cringed. "That's going to be hard to explain, but I'll think of something to get her here. I'll shoot for two o'clock or later, giving you an hour with Dax before she arrives."

Coop nodded. "Sounds good. I'm going try to see the old CFO, a guy named Huck who lives in Brentwood this morning, if I can get in touch with him." He explained about the research into the company. "The current CFO is a guy named Gavin Pierce who has been the CFO of Frank's insurance company since it started. If you have time, dig into him a little and see what you can find out."

Her brow creased. "I've seen that name before. I'll check it out." She took her notepad and cup of tea and went back to her desk.

Coop picked up the phone and punched in the number for Huck. A robotic voice invited him to leave a message. He did so and left his cell number asking Huck to return his call.

Dax arrived a few minutes early, his eyes wide with hope above his clean-shaven face, and AB ushered him back to Coop's office. Coop gestured to the chair in front of his desk. "We've got some promising news."

He explained about the bit of deception they employed at the beauty salon. Coop pointed at the copy of the test results. "They need a paternal sample to come to a conclusive result."

Dax nodded his understanding and then blew out a breath. "I'm not sure Dad will believe me, but I'm willing to meet with him and ask him."

Coop tapped his pen on his notebook. "AB called Lindsay, and she'll be here in less than an hour. We thought it might be easiest for you to reunite with her first, and we can help you explain things. We hope she can serve as a bridge to your dad." Dax popped his knuckles and grinned. "I'm excited, but nervous at the same time. I hated leaving Lindsay and have been wishing for this day for so long, but it's also a little scary." He pointed at his watch. "I'm hoping she remembers this watch that Mom gave me for graduation."

"Honestly, that's why we did the DNA collection before we set up a meeting with the two of you. My gut tells me what you've said happened is the truth, but I didn't want to subject Lindsay to a scam. The test helped bolster my feelings. I hope she's excited to see you, but I'm sure it will come as a major shock, so try to be prepared for a negative reaction."

Dax nodded and reached for the tea AB had thoughtfully delivered. "I'm sure she won't want to believe Dad had any part of all this. I know I didn't either, but at this stage, I need to know the truth, no matter how painful it is."

The phone atop Coop's desk rang, and he reached for the receiver. "I'll come out and speak with her and then bring her back or have you come and get Dax. Thanks, AB."

He turned to Dax. "Ready? I'll go chat with her, and then we'll introduce you in a few minutes."

Dax swallowed hard and nodded, his hands gripping the mug of tea.

Coop wandered down the hallway with Gus following him. He smiled at the brunette woman standing in the reception area. Coop relaxed when he noticed the penetrating blue eyes meeting his. They were identical to Dax's.

He extended his hand. "Thanks so much for coming, Ms. Covington. I know this is unusual." Dressed in a chic sweater dress and boots, along with a blue cape that matched her eyes, she looked like she had stepped out of the pages of a fashion magazine.

Her eyes widened as she gestured toward AB. "Your assistant told me it was something to do with my father and his estate, and you thought it best to talk to me since you knew he was ill. I'm still confused but am curious."

He suggested she take a seat on the couch, and he took a chair next to it. "This is going to come as a shock, I know. Rest assured, we've done everything we can to vet the information I'm going to share with you. I wouldn't have asked you here if I didn't think it was trustworthy."

Her forehead creased in confusion as she accepted the cup of tea AB had brewed for her.

"I know you were only ten when your brother Dax was killed. This is the part that will be difficult. My client is Dax Covington. He came in the office last week and explained what had happened twenty-five years ago and that everyone thought he died in the fire, but he didn't." Coop ignored Lindsay's gasp and continued, "He's anxious to reconnect with you and explain more about what happened. He's waiting in my office."

Her head shook as she tried to set her mug on the coffee table, her hands trembling. "This can't be true. We had a funeral and buried him next to my mother. I remember all of that. It was horrific."

"I know this isn't easy to understand or believe." He gestured to AB, and she stepped down the hallway to his office. "I want you to meet Dax, and I do believe he is your brother but seeing him and talking to him might help."

Tears fell onto her pale cheeks. "I... I... don't know."

Coop patted her arm. "AB and I will be right here with you."

Moments later, Dax stepped into the reception area and came around the coffee table to stand in front of Lindsay. Tears filled his eyes. "Linds, it's me. It's Dax."

She tilted her head, and her lips disappeared as she gazed at him. He skirted the coffee table and moved closer to her. Coop encouraged him with a nod of his head.

"I want to tell you everything, but first I have to tell you how sorry I am I left you. I was scared and didn't know what to do. May I sit next to you?"

She didn't say a word but gestured to the cushion next to her, as her entire body trembled.

As he sat, she reached for his left arm and focused on the watch. Dax grinned and said, "I was hoping you would remember it. Mom gave it to me for graduation."

A fresh round of tears spilled onto Lindsay's cheeks, and AB retrieved a box of tissues for her. "I remember, but this doesn't make sense. I went to your funeral. I put flowers on your grave on your birthday and holidays. I can't believe you were alive all this time." Her shoulders shook as her voice cracked and turned into sobs. She stared into Dax's eyes. "It is you, isn't it?"

A single tear slid down Dax's cheek. "Yes, Linds. It's really me. Ask me anything you want." He reached for her hand, and she took it.

Coop cleared his throat and explained when Dax learned the fire was attributed to a faulty pilot light and a propane explosion, he believed someone had tried to kill him. "He had uncovered some evidence that pointed to wrongdoing on the part of Royal Amusement in the horrible accidents that claimed the lives of several children. He had called and left a message for your dad, telling him that and that he was on his way home. He had just given his RV to a young man named Nate that same afternoon. It was Nate who was killed in the fire. Dax had left his wallet behind and was on his way back to retrieve it when he saw the aftermath of the fire and chose to go into hiding."

Lindsay slumped against the back of the couch. She kept shaking her head. "None of this makes sense." She turned to look at Dax. "Why didn't you just call Dad again and tell him?"

Dax sighed. "I was afraid he was the one who tried to kill me.

He was the only person I called and told what I had discovered and where I was. I just thought I'd be safer if everyone thought it was me in the fire."

She grimaced, mascara trails streaking her cheeks. "Dad would never want to kill you. That's crazy. Are you sure it wasn't an accident and all this, these last twenty-five years were a mistake?"

Dax shrugged. "That's why I'm here. At the time, I thought running away was my only option. All I knew was I called Dad to tell him about the evidence and the next day, my trailer exploded. That RV was old, but it was safe, and I never had a problem. I still don't think it was an accident. When I saw the newspaper article about Dad marrying his secretary, I wondered about everything. About Mom. About the fire. All of it. The company was Dad's life, so while I didn't want to believe it, I couldn't take a chance. I was only twenty and had nobody to turn to."

She dabbed at her face with a tissue. "Losing Mom and then you, it was like living in a nightmare. It took me years to feel normal. Honestly, I'm not sure I've ever felt normal again. Where have you been all this time?"

Dax told her about the little village in Cornwall where he lived and worked. "I kept up with the newspaper online and saw the dedication at Vanderbilt and Dad said he was sick and dying. I decided I couldn't wait any longer. I had to know."

Lindsay's gut-wrenching sobs made Coop's chest ache. "In cases like this, it's impossible to redo the past or dissect every move. Dax came to us because he wants to get to the truth and speak with your dad before it's too late. It might be best if you two spend some time together and reconnect before we set up a meeting with your dad and ultimately a DNA test. We'll need your help to do that Lindsay, when you're ready. Until then, Dax's appearance here needs to remain confidential. None of us can be sure what happened, and we don't want to jeopardize his safety."

AB nodded. "It appears you have no doubt Dax is your brother, is that right?"

Lindsay gazed into Dax's eyes. "I know he's my brother. I'm just not sure I can ever forgive him."

6

F riday morning, Coop slid into his favorite booth at Peg's,
across from Ben. His friend took one look at Coop's shirt,
AGE IS NO GUARANTEE OF MATURITY emblazoned on the chest and
laughed. "Spot on, my friend. Spot on."

Over pecan waffles studded with bits of bacon and a side of
scrambled eggs, Coop brought Ben up to date on the strange
cold case that had walked through his door last week. "Needless
to say, we haven't made much progress on your box of cases."

Ben shrugged. "Not to worry. They're not going anywhere."
He passed the thin file across the table. "Here's what I received
from Georgia. Not much. You can keep these copies."

Coop drummed his fingers on the folder. "It's going to be
hard to find any evidence from twenty-five years ago. I'm
hoping the old guy will just confess, since he's ill. Maybe he'll
want to get it off his chest."

"That's got to be beyond crappy to think your dad tried to
kill you and then to come back and have to convince your
family you're alive. I can't imagine being in Dax's shoes at such a
young age and trying to figure out what to do." Ben accepted the
refill of his coffee from Myrtle.

Coop took a large gulp from his own cup so there was room for a healthy splash from the fresh pot and shook his head. "Families are always more complicated on the inside than they appear from the outside. My mom, for instance... don't even get me started. Having my dad around has been nice this last month. After listening to Dax and his sister yesterday, I decided Dad and I are going out for pizza and brews tonight. I'm lucky to have him."

"It's tough being so far away, I know. Jen struggles with living here and having her family in the Pacific Northwest. I'm lucky my parents are close by."

"I'd say we both have it pretty easy compared to Dax. Neither of us has a dad who we think could kill us."

Coop spent the rest of the morning going over the notes from the fire investigation. As he read through the reports, he slipped the small bag of peanut M&Ms from his drawer and ate them, savoring the weekly treat. Ever since his last bout in the hospital, he had been much better about limiting his intake of nuts and coffee but couldn't bring himself to exclude them entirely.

The county where the deadly fire occurred was small and didn't have a medical examiner or sophisticated crime lab analysis. They did find Dax's wallet and were able to obtain his name from it and the registration of the RV. The detectives on the case showed Dax's photo to the workers and Rex Fitch, the carnival boss, and they all confirmed the man they knew as Johnny Green was Dax Covington.

There was nothing left of the remains to identify, barring a forensic dental analysis, and there was no question from their interviews with everyone onsite that it was indeed Dax, who had been living in the trailer. The initial theory about the pilot light and subsequent ignition of the propane, which would have filled the RV in little time, was listed as the official cause and ruled an accident. It turns out propane leaks are often the cause of fires in motorhomes and newer models have more safety features than the one Dax had purchased.

With it deemed an accidental death, the case was closed once the fire investigation was completed. The police had interviewed Frank, and he stated he didn't know his son was working at the carnival site. He thought he was spending the summer with friends and confirmed Dax's purchase of the RV. He was confused as to why he had been traveling with the division from Royal Amusement but could only guess Dax was hoping to find out more about the accidents, which along with the loss of his mother had impacted him greatly.

Without a question as to the identity of the dead male, who was close enough to the age and build of Dax, and with the remains of Dax's wallet and identification, the county didn't waste money on further analysis. Coop was sure the thought of it being someone other than Dax never entered their minds.

Along with convincing Frank Covington that Dax was indeed alive and that his son suspected him of being behind the fire in his trailer, Coop would have to ask him to exhume the remains so they could go about trying to identify the young man Dax knew as Nate. This was going to become a paperwork nightmare for Ben and for the authorities in Georgia.

Coop keyed Rex Fitch's information into the computer, only to learn he had passed away three years ago. He added his last address to his notepad and scribbled down his relatives in case he needed to interview them. The report also included the names of a few of the carnival workers they had interviewed. Coop scanned the short list and hoped they were findable. Perhaps they were old enough to have retired from a life on the road and had permanent addresses now.

After lunch, Dax called. He had moved into Lindsay's guest room, and they had been talking over the last couple of days, and things had improved since their visit at Coop's office. He let Coop know that Lindsay didn't work and suffered from an anxiety disorder. Her dad supported her, and they were quite close. Lindsay had invited their dad to lunch on Saturday. She didn't tell him anything, just that she wanted him to come and that it was important.

Dax wanted Coop and AB to be there to help explain things. "I hate to ask you to work the weekend, but I'm anxious to confront my dad and see what he has to say."

With AB sitting across the conference table from him, Coop scribbled notes as he listened. He turned the notepad toward her and circled his question about her availability tomorrow. She nodded her agreement.

"That's no problem, Dax. We can both be there and can come early to discuss things before your dad arrives. We'll see you at ten thirty tomorrow." He disconnected and turned back to the glass board behind the conference table.

AB had added information about the parents who had lost children in the earlier accidents. She was trying to pinpoint their activities on the date of the fire. As she reviewed more documents, she discovered that day of the fire was the same date on the depositions the insurance company attorneys had taken. Coop was relieved they had an alibi. The last thing he wanted to do was dredge up the horrible memories of the accidents. The three accidents had taken place in small towns in Kansas and Missouri, too far away from Georgia to facilitate a quick trip.

AB arched her brows as she studied the compilation of their notes. "As awkward as it will be to be there when Dax meets his father, it will speed things along and start the ball rolling on the DNA test and the exhumation. I'll give Ben a head's up, so he can get that process started."

Coop pointed at Nate's name. "I haven't had any luck finding a missing person report from that time for anyone named Nathan or Nate, but Ben will have more resources for that. It's heartbreaking to think his family has been missing him all this time. I know his death weighs on Dax. If his dad is responsible, I'm not sure what will happen between the two of them."

"I was glad Lindsay didn't question Dax's identity. She seemed convinced from the first words he spoke to her. I think the conversation with his dad won't be quite as easy." AB sighed and took a sip from her cup.

Coop grimaced. "An understatement, for sure."

Saturday morning, Coop met AB in the driveway of a beautiful Federal-style brick home, with manicured ivy covering most of the front. Lindsay's house was less than a mile from Aunt Camille's and from the research Coop had done, Frank's home was just about four miles away in the other direction.

They both took a deep breath, and Coop rang the bell. Lindsay greeted them with a pleasant smile and led them through the entry to a sunroom, filled with light from the three walls of windows.

Dax rose from the couch and greeted them with a hearty handshake. "Thanks for coming. I'm nervous and appreciate your help and having you here."

Moments later, Lindsay reappeared with a tray bearing coffee and tea. The aroma was too much for Coop to resist, and he helped himself to a cup of the fresh brew, ignoring the squinty eye AB gave him.

After his first sip, Coop turned toward Lindsay. "How is your dad doing? Do you think he can handle seeing Dax, health-wise?"

She nodded. "He's a pretty tough cookie. Today is a great day for him to visit, because his wife Adele is out of town and she can be… dramatic. She focuses on Dad's illness, to his detriment. He's much stronger when she's not around."

AB patted the leather bag she carried. "If we can get him to agree to a DNA test, we can do the collections here and get them to the lab right away." She glanced at Coop and continued, "Speaking of Adele, is it correct that her son Gavin Pierce is the CFO of your dad's company?"

Lindsay nodded. "That's right. He's worked with Dad since he graduated college, first at Royal and now at the new company."

AB consulted her notepad. "And your dad and Adele married as planned, about two months after the fire, right?"

"Yes, and then she cut back on work and took care of me, just working a few hours in the morning and eventually stayed home. At the time, I didn't really understand what was happening and was devastated after Dax…" She reached for her cup. "It was a small wedding at the house right around Thanksgiving."

Coop met Dax's eyes. "I would imagine it's going to take some time for your dad to get over the initial shock of seeing you. I'd like to broach the subject of an exhumation soon. Along with figuring out what happened, we need to also do our best to identify Nate and bring closure to his family."

Dax nodded, and Lindsay's eyes glistened with a fresh sheen. "Linds and I have been talking about that same thing. Along with leaving Lindsay, having him perish is among my biggest regrets at running away."

Lindsay set her saucer and cup on the coffee table. "We'll do everything we can to find his identity and help his family. I know what it's like to live with the loss of those you love; having Dax back home is something I never imagined. It's like a true miracle. If I had suffered with not knowing what had happened to him, like Nate's family must have, it would have been worse.

The not knowing and imagining horrible things would be awful."

Coop finished off his coffee and placed the empty cup on the table. "We'll see how it goes today, but we'll need to ask your dad some rather pointed questions about his involvement in the falsification of the maintenance records, the accidents, and the fire that killed Nate. I can do that without you present, if that's easier."

Lindsay shook her head and reached for her brother's hand. "No, we talked about it, and we're prepared for whatever we learn. Dax needs to know the truth and so do I. About everything."

The chime of the doorbell interrupted their conversation. Lindsay startled at the sound of it. Dax stepped outside onto the brick patio as they had planned, and she hurried to the front door. Moments later, she ushered in a tall, thin man, dressed in a button-down shirt and blazer. Coop noticed he darted his soft blue eyes behind his glasses around the room.

Lindsay kept her arm looped through her dad's while Coop stood and extended his hand. "Mr. Covington, I'm Cooper Harrington and this is my associate, Annabelle Davenport."

"Call me Frank, please," he said, shaking Coop's hand and nodding across the room at AB. "You must be related to Camille?"

Coop smiled. "Yes, sir. She's my aunt, and I went to school here at Vanderbilt and lived with her and Uncle John. I loved them and Nashville so much, I never left. When my uncle passed away, I took over his agency. I'm a private detective and lawyer, and my latest client is why I'm here today."

Frank's smile faded, and he took a seat in the chair next to Coop. Lindsay poured her dad a cup of coffee and handed it to him before she slipped back into her spot on the couch.

Coop took his seat and cleared his throat. "We met with Lindsay this week and explained a situation that involves you and your family, and she's had a few days to come to grips with it and arranged this meeting so we could help answer any questions you have. We know this will come as a shock, but your son Dax, who everyone believed died twenty-five years ago, is alive."

Frank shook his head as he struggled to place his cup on the saucer and sloshed coffee from the rim. "That can't be. This is some horrible trick. Lindsay?" His eyes pleaded with her, and he gripped the arm of the chair, as if he were ready to leave.

She stood and tried to smile at her father, as tears shimmered in her eyes. "It's true, Daddy. I've talked to him, and it's Dax. He has the watch Mom gave him for graduation. She stepped to the door leading to the patio and cracked it open, motioning Dax to come inside.

Her brother stepped over the threshold, his face pale, as he locked eyes with his father. "Dad, it's me."

Frank darted his eyes from Dax to Lindsay and then to Coop. "This is ridiculous. Dax died in a horrible fire. Why are you doing this?"

Dax stepped closer to his dad. "Ask me anything, Dad. I'm not a fraud. I remember the special bowtie you wore to my high school graduation, the one you ordered in silver and cardinal to match my school colors and the new dress Mom wore in the same red. I remember when you and Mom brought Lindsay home from the hospital and let me hold her and how you hovered over me to make sure I didn't drop her."

He licked his lips and glanced at his sister. "I remember Lindsay's last birthday before Mom died. You gave her a gold necklace with her name written in cursive and a little diamond above it." He sighed. "I remember Mom's funeral and the pink dress we picked out for her to wear."

Tears streamed down Frank's cheeks. He took a handkerchief out of his pocket and dabbed his eyes. In a voice barely above a whisper, he said, "I don't understand. I can't believe this."

Dax sat in a chair closer to his dad, while Coop addressed Frank, "There's simply no easy way to do this, and we know it's difficult to take all this in. Let me try to summarize what happened twenty-five years ago. Then I know Dax would be happy to answer any specific questions."

Coop went through the events the led up to that fateful day twenty-five years ago, including Dax posing as a laborer with the hope of getting to the bottom of the accidents plaguing Royal Amusement and him giving Nate his old RV and job. "Frank, did you get a voicemail on your office phone from Dax the day before the fire?"

Confusion filled his eyes, and he frowned, looking from Dax to Coop, shaking his head. "No, I didn't get a message or talk to Dax."

Coop glanced at Dax and then turned his eyes on Frank. "This next part will be difficult to hear, but Dax left you a voicemail the day before the fire. He wanted you to know he had evidence of false records and skipped maintenance on the carnival rides. All his work led him to believe someone at the corporate office was directing the carnival bosses to skimp and falsify the logs to save money. Rex had made notes in his personal notebook about it, and Dax nosed around with the carnies enough to verify most of it." Coop noticed Frank's eyes widen, and he shook his head.

"Dax was on his way home, having bought a motorcycle, when he realized he had left his wallet in the RV and went back to retrieve it. That's when he happened upon the fire and subsequently learned he was presumed dead. Since you were the only person who knew where he was and what he was doing, he feared you had rigged the explosion to kill him and bury the information that would implicate the company and you in the cause of the fatal accidents."

A low moan escaped from Frank. It sounded like a wounded animal and prompted both AB and Lindsay to rush to his chair.

He waved them both away, and Lindsay retreated to the kitchen to get him a glass of cold water.

After a few swallows and several moments of silence, Frank finally spoke, "The only thing worse than having my son dead is knowing he believes I could kill him." His body shook, racked with sobs.

7

With it clear Frank believed Dax to be his son, Coop asked about a DNA test. After several moments of staring at Dax, Frank agreed to it, and AB swabbed his and Lindsay's cheek before she and Coop gave the three of them some time alone. Lindsay had ordered food for lunch, and Coop and AB went about setting it up on the huge island counter in the well-appointed kitchen, while they left the family together in the sunroom.

AB unwrapped the sandwich tray and fruit platter and whispered to Coop, "What's your first impression?"

"Frank seems genuinely sad and surprised. I think Dax's descriptions of his memories convinced him he is his son."

She nodded and placed a bowl of salad next to the sandwiches. Coop found another tray and much to his delight, discovered it contained stacks of freshly baked cookies.

He swiped one before AB could bat his hand away. He grinned and took a bite. "We'll have to dig in a bit more and ask some pointed questions. It's hard doing that to a guy who is frail and sick."

"It's also difficult with Lindsay and Dax here, but they said they wanted to stick around." She shrugged and poured glasses of sweet tea. There was a breakfast nook off the kitchen with a wall of windows overlooking the backyard. In summer, it would be a gorgeous view and despite it being January, it was still lovely. Lindsay had the table set, and the vase of fresh flowers gave it a cheerful look.

AB surveyed the counter and raised her brows. "I'll go tell them soup's on."

Moments later, the three of them filed into the kitchen with Frank's arm linked in Lindsay's. He looked much weaker than when he had arrived. She got him situated in a chair and offered to fill his plate for him. He gazed out the window and said, "Not too much. I'm not very hungry."

Coop made sure to take the seat across from Frank, so he could watch his reactions as they chatted. While they ate, Lindsay teased information from Dax about his life in Cornwall, and he shared a few stories of his life as a pub manager.

Coop didn't want to prevent Frank from eating, so he held his questions until the plates had been cleared, and the cookies and coffee had been added to the table. Coop wouldn't meet AB's eyes as he accepted a fresh cup of coffee and another cookie.

After his first sip, he placed the cup back on the saucer. "Frank, I know this has been more than a shock to you, and I don't relish upsetting you further, but there are some questions we need to ask you. I'll admit, this is a bit unusual, in that Lindsay and Dax said they wanted to be here for the interview. If, at any time, you wish to stop and prefer we meet alone, just let me know."

He nodded and clasped his hands in front of him, resting them on the table.

Coop consulted his notepad and then looked across the table at Frank. "I've read through the police report and fire investigation. You stated you didn't know Dax was posing as a worker at the carnival site in Georgia, is that correct?"

"That's right. I was shocked when I got the call from the authorities." He glanced at his son. "Dax told me he was going to spend the summer with friends, traveling across the country in that old RV he bought."

Coop frowned. "So, what could have happened to the message he left you the day before? Dax called your direct line from a payphone."

Frank shook his head. "I never received that message. I didn't know anything about what he suspected."

"Who had access to your messages?"

"I had one of those answering machines on my desk. It wasn't all fancy and automated like nowadays. My office was open to everyone who worked there." His eyes moved up, in thought. "Well, Adele, who was my secretary at the time, of course. Then, there was Huck; he was the CFO. Gavin, who worked with Huck. Also Marvin, who was the head of sales and bookings. Then any number of clerks who helped in the accounting and sales offices. I didn't keep it locked or anything."

"Gavin is Adele's son, correct?"

"Yes. When he graduated business school, I gave him a job working with Huck. He was educated but needed to learn the ropes in the real world. I was hoping he would work alongside Huck and then be able to slide into his position when Huck retired, down the road."

Coop frowned. "Huck left before you sold the company, though, is that right?"

Frank's lips thinned. "Yes, he left right after the fire in Georgia and Dax." He took a sip of the sweet tea he hadn't finished. "He had been unhappy for months and ended up leaving us for a job in Memphis. I needed him and relied on him but understood he had a great opportunity. It did surprise me, though. He had been with me from the beginning."

Coop jotted something on the pad. "You sold the company less than a year later. Why did you decide to do that?"

Frank leaned back and sighed. "Too many sad memories. Big Top had been trying to get me to sell to them for years. They were our closest competitor and after losing Laura Beth and then Dax, I just couldn't go on. I needed to start fresh and get away from the sadness and the memories."

Coop nodded. "I know it was a long time ago, but can you think of anyone who wanted to harm you or your business? Anyone who could have been involved in the accidents that plagued your company?"

Frank's hands trembled. "At the time, I thought Big Top may have been involved, as in trying to sabotage us, get us to sell, whatever. It even crossed my mind someone in Royal could have been working with them, maybe facilitating it so they could buy us out." He shook his head, like he was trying to shake off bad memories. "It pained me, but Huck was someone I suspected. As I said, he wasn't happy and didn't get on with Gavin, but I can't imagine him going to those lengths."

Coop glanced at Dax and Lindsay, both of whom focused on their father. Dax was calm, and Lindsay rubbed her hands together. He returned his attention to Frank. "This will sound indelicate, but Dax said when he saw the article in the paper about his death in the fire, there was an accompanying piece about you announcing your engagement to Adele. It seemed fast to him and led him to question if you were involved with her prior to your wife's death."

Tears glistened in the old man's eyes, and he turned and looked at his children. "Adele had always been attentive, overly sometimes. She had made it clear she was available in a romantic way, but I never crossed the line. I should have been more forceful with her, but I just chalked it up to her being lonely. She was a wonderful secretary and kept things running smoothly when I was in no position to function."

He took a deep breath. "With Laura Beth gone and Dax in school and starting his own life, Lindsay needed a mother. Adele was more than willing and convenient and fit into my life easily. It wasn't some torrid love affair at all; it was more a matter of practicality and my desire to have someone with Lindsay. She was so young and desperate for her mother. I hoped Adele could fill that void. For her. For me."

Frank looked at his children, meeting their eyes. "I never cheated on your mother. She was the love of my life."

Tears snaked down Lindsay's cheeks, and her lips quivered. Dax swallowed hard, and his jaw tensed as he listened to his father speak.

Frank looked across the table at Coop. "It sounds awful now, but I wouldn't go anywhere to meet another woman and hadn't even come to terms with losing my wife, then Dax…" He shifted in the chair. "Adele seemed like the best solution, and she's a lovely woman. A couple of years older than me, but you wouldn't know it by looking at her." His lips turned into a quick smile. "I'm glad she's not here to hear me say it that way. We've had a nice life, and she's a wonderful woman, but my heart will always belong to Laura Beth."

Coop looked down at his notes. "And Adele's first husband died?"

Frank nodded. "Long ago, when Gavin was young. She reverted to her maiden name, Adele West. I'm not sure the exact year he died, but it was before she came to work for me."

"When is she due home?" asked Coop.

"Thursday. She's on a trip with a couple of friends to Florida. We have a place on Clearwater Beach. I usually go but didn't feel like traveling right now, so I urged her to go ahead. She needs a break."

"I'll be interviewing her and Gavin, along with Huck and Marvin. I'd ask that you not divulge Dax's return or our conversation. It's best if I can ask the questions and get first impressions without having anyone prepare for the interview." He glanced at Lindsay. "Same goes for you, too."

Frank slowly nodded his head and made a triangle with his index fingers and thumbs. "I understand that. I have nothing to hide and want more than anything for you to get to the bottom of all this. With so much time passed, I'm not sure it's possible, but spare no expense. I'll cover the costs of whatever you're doing for Dax. It's the least I can do."

"Thank you. We've been cognizant of Dax's situation and have tried to keep our expenses to a minimum. I found Huck's information, but if you have any idea on Marvin's whereabouts or remember the names of anyone else who worked in the office at the time of the fire, let us know."

"Marvin Eastman was his name, and he may have gone to work for Big Top. I'm not sure where he ended up. He wasn't interested in selling insurance and didn't join us in the new company. The payroll clerk was Bethany something. She also didn't move with us, as we didn't have a large staff of employees that needed paying. I'll go into the office tomorrow and look through any old files we may have kept. Adele might be able to help when she gets home, or Gavin."

AB brought her notebook and slid into the empty chair next to Frank. "I'll take down those names and if you have Gavin's contact information, we can get started with his interview first."

She wrote down information while Frank, who looked more drawn and tired by the minute, looked on his phone and gave her Gavin's contact information.

Lindsay stood and put a hand on her dad's shoulder. "How about I drive you home? I think a rest would do you good."

He patted her hand. "I could definitely do with a nap, sweetheart. I'll let Dax drive me, though. He can spend some time at the house, and maybe we can chat more after I've rested." His eyes found his son's. "I've also never been able to part with that old Mustang you loved. It's still in the garage and probably in need of some maintenance."

Dax's eyes widened. "You still have it? I can't believe it." He grinned and for the first time since meeting him, Coop caught a glimpse of what Dax must have been like as a young man.

As he watched Dax gently and longingly help his dad from the chair and place his arm around his shoulders as he led him to the door, something deep inside Coop fluttered. He hoped Frank wasn't responsible for the accidents or the fire that killed Nate.

Twenty-five years was a long time. Memories faded, people died or moved, evidence was lost or degraded. If only Dax had come home sooner, Coop's job would be easier.

8

Saturday night, after a short nap, Coop slipped into his favorite boots and the soft, blue, button-down shirt he liked. He left Gus curled up with Aunt Camille, who was busy finding a movie she knew Charlie would like.

"You kids enjoy yourselves," said Charlie with a wave.

Coop drove downtown to Houston's, where AB would meet him. The hostess led him to a corner booth, and as soon as he sat, the waitstaff poured two waters and deposited a basket of warm bread and salted butter on the table. Coop was intrigued with the tin can that housed fresh cornbread, and the smell of the rosemary herb bread made his stomach growl.

As he contemplated how rude it would be to cut a slice, AB appeared. Coop's eyes widened and took in the shimmery off-the-shoulder sweater she wore that matched her blue-green eyes perfectly. She was also wearing jeans and boots but had done something different with her hair; the soft, effortless waves suited her.

He stood as she slid into her side of the booth. AB never wore much makeup and was a casual dresser at work, but Coop noticed she had taken extra care tonight. The soft dusting of eyeshadow and a hint of color on her lips accentuated her natural beauty. "You look lovely, AB."

She cocked her head and smiled. "Well, thank you. It's not often that I get to go out for a fifteen-hundred-dollar meal." She winked and took a sip of water.

Coop sliced the bread, and they perused the menu. It didn't take long for him to decide on the ribeye, and AB opted for the filet. As they waited for their soup, Coop sliced more bread.

"So, what did you learn from staying behind today and talking with Lindsay while I dealt with Janice and convinced her to meet me at the lab so I could drop the samples off on a Saturday?"

She snickered while she slathered butter onto the warm cornbread. "Despite my usual distrust of beautiful women born with a silver spoon, she's quite nice. She talked about her incessant anxiety and how it's kept her from so many things. She started an event planning business a few years ago but couldn't handle it because it stressed her too much. She's quite close to her dad and concerned about him. She's thrilled that Dax is back. Told me she has to pinch herself to make sure it isn't a dream."

The waiter returned with butternut squash soup for each of them. AB added pepper to hers and waited for it to cool a bit. "Lindsay is worried about her dad but was glad he was receptive to Dax. She said there's no question as to his identity. She talked a little about her mom and how that was the first time her dad divulged he had married Adele, in a large part, to take care of her. I got the feeling Adele was kind but smothering."

Coop nodded as he took his first spoonful of soup. "I had the same feeling just listening to what they said today. I want to talk to her before she knows anything about Dax's return. Same with her son Gavin. That'll be hard to do, but the sooner the better."

"She's in Clearwater Beach; it's only an hour and thirty-minute flight to Tampa. Maybe you should just fly down and talk to her."

Coop's brows arched, and he grinned at her. "Genius idea. Let's interview Gavin early tomorrow and then take a quick trip down there. Nothing like an escape to Florida in January to take away the winter blues."

As they dug into their tender steaks and sampled the black truffle butter sauce and bacon chutney, the trip to Florida solidified. AB pulled out her phone and booked them two tickets for tomorrow afternoon. She remembered the name of the condo in Clearwater Frank had given her and looked it up on the map. They could conduct the interview and be back Monday afternoon.

By the time they finished the sumptuous meal and waited on desserts, she had booked two rooms at the resort next to Frank and Adele's condo and arranged a shuttle from the airport. "Shall I just put a message on the recorder and a note on the door that we're closed Monday?"

Coop leaned back. "I'll see if Dad and Aunt Camille want to babysit the place. They'd probably enjoy it and can just take messages and call us with anything important."

"Even better," she said with a grin. The waiter set the crème brulee and chocolate cake with ice cream, both of which were covered in bourbon caramel sauce in the middle of the table.

AB eyed the decadent desserts and shook her head. "Oh, man. I'm not sure I can eat anything else. I'm stuffed."

"Aww, come on, AB. Just a bite or two. We can't let it go to waste." Coop slid a spoon into the crème brulee and shut his eyes as he tasted it. "Mmm, that's so good."

She took several bites from each dessert and called it quits. "I'm done. If I have any hope of line dancing, I have to stop."

"Oh, I forgot about that. You're right. I need to stop, or I won't be able to walk out of here, much less dance." He shook his head and pushed the plate with the cake away from him. "I'm not much on dancing anyway."

Her eyes narrowed. "You promised. We had a deal, remember?"

He held up a hand. "I know, I know. I'll do it. I'm just warning you."

The waiter offered coffee or tea, and they each opted for a cup of tea before they made their way to the other side of the huge restaurant and the dance floor.

The band was superb, as was the woman leading the dancing. The talented group played current and past country hits, which were made for dancing. AB was a natural and had no trouble following the steps, but Coop took a bit longer to find his rhythm. Once he relaxed and mastered a couple of songs, he was surprised at how much he enjoyed it. It had been years, more like decades, since he had spent time line dancing. It had been a popular weekend activity when he was in college, and he had forgotten how much fun it was.

Before they knew it, they had been dancing for hours, and it was close to midnight when they called it a night. "How about we meet at the Donut Hole in the morning, and we can strategize for the interview?"

"Works for me," said AB as he helped her into her coat. "We can take my car and leave it at the airport overnight. I'll pick you up at the house in the morning."

He saw her to her car and waved as she pulled away from the parking lot. Coop slid behind the wheel of his Jeep, feeling more relaxed than he had in weeks. Maybe the night on the town and all the dancing would prove to be a sleep inducer. He could only hope. Tomorrow would be a long day, and he needed the rest.

∽

Early the next morning, Coop tossed his overnight bag on the backseat and folded himself into the passenger seat of AB's car, groaning as he shifted to attach his seatbelt. "I think line dancing is more exercise than I thought. I'm sore all over."

AB chuckled. "Yeah, my legs are a little sore, but not terrible."

She parked next to the Donut Hole, and they grabbed one of the coveted booths in the back. Coop returned with a box of assorted donuts and two large cups of coffee. He gave her first pick and then chose one of the maple-frosted donuts covered with bits of candied bacon. "I think we should get in touch with Frank and let him know we'll be using his name as our client when we talk to Gavin, Adele, and anyone else associated with Royal Amusement. The story of Dax's return is so sensational, it will overshadow everything else. It also begs to be shared, and I'd rather not have that publicized, as I'm sure the family would agree. They can share that story as they see fit."

AB nodded as she took a sip from her cup. "That makes sense. Depending how it goes with Gavin and Adele, we could share Dax's return toward the end of the interview. I think it might be interesting to see how they respond to the news but agree Frank's name will open the doors for us. But if we start with Dax, the shock will be overwhelming, and they would be apt to disbelieve it anyway."

Coop finished off another donut and put in a call to Frank's home. Coop explained they wanted to use his name as their client, and he didn't hesitate to agree. When Coop disconnected, he arched his brows at AB. "That was easy. He said if anyone has a question, to tell them to contact him, and he'll vouch for us."

AB finished her coffee and slid out of the booth. "Let's head to Franklin and call Gavin when we're close, so we keep the element of surprise on our side."

Coop grinned and tucked the box of leftover donuts under his arm. "I like how you think, AB."

They drove less than twenty minutes to the wealthy neighborhood of Forest Home in Franklin, and AB pulled over when they were about a mile from Gavin's house. Coop dialed Gavin's cell phone and introduced himself, making sure to mention Frank's name. Coop stressed the urgency and apologized for contacting him on a Sunday but was firm that they meet with him now.

Coop nodded as he listened to Gavin. "Great, my associate and I can be there in a few minutes, and we'll make it as quick as possible."

Coop rolled his eyes as soon as he disconnected. "He's got a tee time at ten o'clock." Coop glanced at the dash clock. "We've got plenty of time."

Minutes later, AB guided her VW Bug down the long driveway flanked by white fencing and around the concrete circle in front of the house. It was a sprawling stone ranch, graced by mature trees, set in the midst of a few acres.

Coop rang the bell, and a middle-aged man greeted them. With a high forehead and the dark scruff of whiskers across his cheeks and chin signaling he hadn't shaved all weekend. His dark eyes behind his glasses held a hint of annoyance. He extended his hand. "You must be Mr. Harrington. I'm Gavin Pierce."

"Thanks for seeing us on such short notice, Mr. Pierce. This is my associate Annabelle Davenport."

Annabelle shook his hand, and he smiled at her. "Please come in." He led them across the highly polished wooden floor of the entry into an open living area next to the large kitchen. "I'd offer you coffee, but I'm afraid I just poured the last cup."

Coop held up his hand. "We've had ours but thank you." Not that he had offered them anything. Coop recognized the high-end label on Gavin's golf pants stretched over the paunch of his belly, a matching shirt, and a waterproof jacket. Coop wasn't sure how he ended up on the company's mailing list but knew from perusing their catalog, Gavin's weekend outfit cost well over a thousand dollars.

The house reeked of affluence with the quality leather furnishings, paintings, and artwork that graced the walls, and well-appointed decorative pieces tucked into shelves and corners. It looked like it was staged for a real estate showing; everything looked shiny and pristine, and nothing looked lived in.

Coop pulled out his notepad. "As I explained on the phone, Frank Covington has retained our services to look into the accidents and events at Royal Amusement, including the death of his son Dax at the carnival site in Georgia."

Gavin shook his head and frowned. "I know the old boy isn't long for the world but dredging up ancient history seems like a waste of what little time he has left."

Coop ignored him. "We understand you started working at Royal after you graduated and took a position working in the accounting offices under the CFO Huck Grover, correct?"

He nodded. "That's right. Mom put in a good word for me with Frank. At the time, she was his secretary and had been working there for several years. He hired me and wanted me to learn all I could from Huck." Gavin's chuckle carried a condescending tone. "Huck was a good guy, but old school. Old ideas, and he wasn't too keen on me and my new ideas. We didn't hit it off like Frank thought we would."

Coop scribbled on his pad. "Did you have, or do you now have any theories about the terrible accidents involving the rides that took the lives of those children?"

Gavin shook his head and frowned. "Not really. Just thought it was bad luck, maybe old equipment or something. We pulled all the maintenance logs and everything associated with the equipment, and it all checked out."

Coop asked a few more questions as Gavin explained the maintenance logs were kept onsite with each carnival boss and then copies transmitted to headquarters where they transferred the data into a software program that made it easy to search and track. The system also flagged equipment when maintenance was due.

Coop nodded and looked down at his notes. "What about Big Top? They were a competitor, right?"

Gavin bobbed his head as he swallowed a sip of coffee. "They'd been trying to buy Frank out for several years, from what I understand. Ultimately, they did, so maybe they were behind it, and it worked. I don't know of any actual evidence of that, though. They paid us a fair price when we sold, but our value had diminished because of the accidents, which favored them."

"Did anyone who worked at Royal take a job with Big Top after they acquired the business?"

Gavin nodded. "Oh, yeah. Part of the deal was they had to make sure there were jobs for everyone in the field. Not the casual laborers, but everyone else."

"What about anyone in the corporate office?"

Gavin took a long swallow from his mug. "I'm trying to remember. That was a long time ago. I think the payroll clerk, maybe a couple others who worked in the business office, and I'm not sure about Marvin. He booked locations, so stands to reason he may have been offered a job. I honestly didn't pay that much attention."

Coop put a star next to Bethany's name and a question mark next to Marvin's. "Frank told us the payroll clerk was Bethany. Do you remember her last name?"

"Oh, let me think." He tapped his fingers against the side of his cup. "I reviewed enough of her payroll sheets she signed, I should." After a few moments, he said, "Lewis. It was Bethany Lewis."

Coop nodded. "What about the fire at the carnival site in Georgia. Do you know anything about it?"

He shook his head. "No, only that it was a horrible time. Frank was devastated. Never the same after that happened. Everyone was shocked."

"Do you remember who was the carnival boss at that site? Or any of the workers?"

Gavin laughed. "Really, you think I would remember any of those people after twenty-five years? I doubt I could remember them after a week."

Coop pressed his pen into the notepad with enough force to leave a dent and a large smudge of ink. "Can you think of anyone else who might have wanted to sabotage the company and could have been involved in the fire or the accidents?"

Gavin's substantial forehead creased. "Are you saying Frank thinks those kids dying and the fire weren't accidents?"

Coop shrugged. "We're just looking at all possibilities at this point. Getting as much background for what was happening at the time. Anybody have a grudge against Frank, personal or business?"

"Wow. I can't think of anyone who would go to that length, no matter what the grudge. Like you say, a competitor makes the most sense, but killing people seems extreme."

"Unless they didn't mean to kill anyone? Who was the main person at Big Top who made the offers or that you dealt with at the corporate office?"

"The owner himself, a guy named Red Fulton, from what I know. He was arrogant and unpleasant, but I never took him to be violent."

Coop added another note. "Tell us about the culture at the Royal offices. Was it formal or casual? Did everyone have access to Frank or was he closed off in his office most of the time?"

Gavin squinted as he thought. "I'd say it was pretty casual. We didn't get many walk-in visitors. Mom's office was at the front of the building, and there was a conference room between her office and Frank's. Frank had a second door in his office that led to the back door and to a hallway that fed into the business offices, where I worked, along with Huck and the clerks for accounting and payroll. All the numbers came to us on paper, and we had to input them into the computer, so there were quite a few data entry clerks. Marvin's office was on the other side of our area."

"So, for instance, if you or Huck needed to see Frank, did you have to go through your mom to get an appointment?"

He shook his head. "Oh, no. Nothing like that. Most of the time, we just accessed him through that back door in our hallway. Many times, he left it open and otherwise, we'd just call his extension or knock, and he'd holler for us to come in."

"So, his office was pretty much open to everyone who worked there? It doesn't sound like it was secured all the time."

Gavin nodded. "I'd say that's a fair assessment. If he was in a meeting, it was usually in the conference room, so everyone went back and forth freely, sometimes leaving him a folder of stuff to sign or whatever. Like you said, a casual workplace."

Coop looked at AB, and she nodded. "How about the insurance company? Is that a different environment?"

Gavin's eyebrows rose. "Oh, yeah. Way more formal and business-like. We get many more walk-in clients and have just a handful of employees. A secretary, a few agents, and I handle the finances and also have my license to sell insurance. We do mostly property, casualty, and life insurance products. It's quiet and classy, and quite profitable." He winked and took a sip from his cup.

Coop tapped his pen against his notepad. "So, you're the only employee who followed Frank in the new company?"

"His secretary Vivien came with him, too. After Mom married Frank, she stepped back from work and stayed home for the most part. She's always popping in and out of the office, but no longer works. He didn't need many employees for the new venture. Totally different business model where we keep our overhead and costs low."

Coop stood and handed Gavin his card. "If you think of anything else that may be helpful, please reach out. Oh, one more question. Do you know if Dax called and talked to his father or left him a message the day before the fire?"

The lines in Gavin's forehead deepened. "No, why would I know anything about Dax calling? Did Frank say he talked to him?"

Coop continued to the door. "Thanks for your time today."

AB shook Gavin's hand as they left and wished him a good game of golf.

Once they were on the main road, Coop turned to her. "What did you think?"

"I think he should be a used car salesman. He's slimy and full of himself."

Coop chuckled. "Besides the obvious. He's definitely not emotional or attached to Frank. Talking about Dax's death and the accidents didn't seem to bother him."

AB nodded. "Right. He could have cared less. He also seemed curious about Frank talking to Dax. That was a little weird."

"Agreed. Makes me glad I didn't mention Dax's return yet. I wonder what provisions Frank has made for Gavin?"

AB smirked. "Or what Gavin thinks he has made for him. Family situations with second wives are not always straightfor-ward. I'd love to see his face when he finds out Dax is alive. That might upset the apple cart."

"I have a feeling it will upset the entire produce section when Gavin finds out there's another heir, related by blood, who with Lindsay, will likely get the bulk of Frank's estate. It will be interesting to see what Frank decides to do."

AB drove them to the airport, where they made a makeshift lunch out of a container of cheese and fruit paired with their leftover donuts before they had to board the flight to Tampa. As the plane reached altitude, Coop leaned over and said, "Now, we'll see if Gavin called his mom and let her know about our visit. I hoped by playing down the inquiry about Dax, he'd be less apt to interrupt her trip."

AB leaned back and shut her eyes. "I'm going to take a nap and try to prepare myself for Adele. After meeting her son, I can only imagine what she's like."

9

Once on the ground in Tampa, they took the speedy train to the terminal and found the shuttle that would drive them to Clearwater. It was a gorgeous, sunny day, with a slight breeze that fluttered the palm fronds.

They were the only two people on the shuttle, and the driver made quick work of getting them across the bay to Clearwater and dropping them in front of the large luxury property that housed condos, vacation rentals, and hotel guests, mere steps from the pristine beach. Coop and AB stood outside, under the portico, admiring the view of the endless blue water beyond the white sand.

As they planned, Coop put in a call to Frank. They didn't want Frank to inadvertently tell Adele about the visit, so they elected to contact him when they arrived, hoping he'd smooth the way for Adele to grant them access. After a few minutes of chatting, Coop disconnected.

"He was surprised but said he'd call Adele right away. He also promised not to mention Dax." Coop gestured to the resort next door. "Frank said when we check in, give his name and condo number, and they would put it on his tab. He gets a special price for guests."

AB smiled. "Too bad we can't stay longer." She sighed as she gazed at the ocean. "This is a view I would never grow tired of. Maybe when I retire, I'll move to Florida."

Coop chuckled. "You're never retiring, AB. We go out together. That's our deal."

Coop checked his watch and dialed Adele's cell phone. After a brief conversation, he hit the red button. "Wow. She's not too happy to have us here but said Frank had called. She understood we needed to talk to her today. She's calling down to the front desk now." He walked to the door and reached for the handle, but it opened before he could grab it. A doorman, wearing a polo shirt with the property logo, welcomed them with a friendly smile.

The cool, refrigerated air greeted them as they strolled across the tiled lobby and approached the front desk. Coop gave his name and said they were there to see Adele Covington.

The efficient man behind the desk nodded and pointed to the elevator. "Mrs. Covington is expecting you." He rattled off the apartment number on the seventh floor.

Coop and AB rode the elevator and when they stepped off, they gasped at the stunning view from the large window facing the water. "Wowza, that's gorgeous," said AB.

Coop led the way and knocked on the door. A petite woman, with blonde, wispy hair, so perfectly styled it could have been a wig, opened the door. "Mr. Harrington, I presume?" She greeted them with a friendly smile.

"Yes, ma'am. Thank you for seeing us today. This is my associate Annabelle Davenport."

Adele said nothing as she led them through the impressive apartment and into the living room with a view of the beach from the glass doors that led to the lanai. Adele poured iced water with sliced oranges out of a pitcher and handed each of them a glass before taking her seat. She straightened her perfectly pressed turquoise capri pants and colorful blouse, adjusted the string of pearls around her neck, and positioned her glass on a coaster.

"I must apologize for my curtness on the phone. I'm a bit startled by your visit. I have no idea what's gotten into Frank, but he said you're looking into the accidents from twenty-five years ago. He's never gotten over them. I'm sure it's weighing on his mind in the state he's in. I shouldn't have left him alone." If the skin on her face was capable of moving, Coop was sure her forehead would have creased, but she remained expressionless.

As Frank had laughed about, she didn't look older than her husband and if Coop had to guess, he would have pegged her at least fifteen years younger. Her shiny and all-too-smooth skin made her appear younger, but the dark spots and bulging veins on her wrinkly hands gave away her age. As he took in the fake nails and makeup that had been applied with precision and most likely a spatula, he pictured sweet Aunt Camille and her drawn-on eyebrows. He much preferred the natural look of her wrinkles and smile lines to the plastic face across from him.

Coop took a long drink of the refreshing water and dug out his notepad. "As your husband explained, we're looking into the fatal accidents at Royal Amusement. Do you think they were strictly accidents, or do you think someone may have engineered them to hurt Frank or the company?"

She clutched her literal pearls, rubbing them with the pads of her fingers. "Oh, my heavens, no. All the meddling from the authorities and lawyers for those families, and we never found anything to support any wrongdoing. Ultimately, our insurance paid out, and it was chalked up to accidents. Our maintenance records were spotless. Frank was a stickler for making sure things were serviced and properly maintained."

Coop nodded. "We were thinking more along the lines of

someone taking steps to cause the accident, perhaps to devalue Royal. Someone like Red Fulton from Big Top?"

Her eyes widened. "I can't imagine such a sinister act. Even if true, Red died several years ago. Granted, he was always after Frank to sell. He wanted to have the largest amusement company in the country, but I can't imagine he would take such drastic steps." She shrugged and added, "In the end, Red did get what he wanted, though."

Coop made a note. "Can you think of anyone else that worked at Big Top who is still living and might have some insight?"

She shook her head and took a swallow from her glass. "I'll think on it. They were based in Ohio, maybe Indiana. The only one I ever remember dealing with was Red himself."

As he had asked Gavin, Coop asked Adele about the way the office worked and if people were free to come and go from Frank's office. She confirmed what Gavin had described. "Frank had an open-door policy and treated everyone that worked there like family."

After another sip of cold water, Coop continued, "Frank said he had an answering machine on his desk. Did it require a passcode to access?"

Her eyes shifted upwards. "Hmm, that was so long ago. No, I'm sure it didn't. It wasn't fancy."

"Did he usually retrieve his own messages, or did you transcribe them?"

"Typically, I would take messages for him that came in when he was out of the office, but if someone called his direct line, the messages would be captured on the machine. Sometimes, if he was busy, and there were several, I would help by transcribing them and handling any that I could. Otherwise, I left them for him."

Coop tapped his pen on his notepad. "Did Dax often call his father at work?"

She smiled. "If he did, he would call him on his direct line. He and Lindsay both had that number and were close to their dad. After Laura Beth died, Frank was especially attentive and would drop anything if they needed him. With Dax away at school and then traveling with friends for the summer, I don't think he called him that much. Frank would be the one to ask."

Coop nodded. "Do you know if there was a message from Dax on the machine the day before the fire?"

She blinked and opened her eyes wider. "I don't remember one. Did Frank say he talked to him? I don't remember him saying that at the time. His death was such a shock, and I know part of Frank died with him. I wish he wasn't dwelling on it. We've tried so hard to overcome that time." Her eyes glistened with the sheen of fresh tears.

Coop asked Adele about the people who had worked at the corporate office, and she named the same ones Frank and Gavin had remembered. She did supply the names of two more clerks, Penny who helped Marvin with bookings and Alice, Bethany's assistant in payroll. She struggled to remember last names but promised to think about it.

Coop and AB made eye contact, and the smallest gesture of AB's head let Coop know she agreed it was time. "At the time of the fire, did it ever cross your mind that it wasn't an accident? More to the point, that someone deliberately set out to harm Dax?"

"What? Why would anyone want to harm him?" She set her glass down on the table. "Nobody even knew he was there, and it was a complete shock. To all of us. I know the police and fire authorities investigated it and ruled it an accident. It was awful, but I never heard a whisper of anything else."

With a quick glance at his notes, Coop continued, "Do you remember if anyone was absent from work the day of the fire? Was Frank at work when he got the call?"

Her eyes narrowed, and she stared at the floor. "The office

was closed, and we had worked a little late and were just leaving for dinner. The police came to the office to notify him. We were the only ones there at the time. I couldn't tell you if anyone was absent from work that day. Nothing stands out that I remember."

Coop took a long, slow drink from his glass. "This next bit of information may shock you, Mrs. Covington. I just want you to be prepared." She nodded to him, darting her eyes between Coop and AB. "Dax didn't die in that fire. Someone else was in his trailer, and Dax arrived in Nashville last week. He and your husband are working together to try to figure out what happened, and Dax is convinced he was targeted."

Adele's chest and neck bloomed with color that traveled up and into her cheeks. "I, uh, I don't understand. You're... are you telling me Dax is alive?"

"Yes, ma'am. He's staying with Lindsay, and both she and Frank are convinced it's him. They've all taken a DNA test to prove it."

Her hands trembled as she fiddled with the buttons on her blouse. "That's simply unbelievable. I mean, never in a million years, would I have..." She left the sentence unfinished.

Moments later, her hand grabbed at her necklace again. "Are you certain it isn't just some grifter taking advantage of Frank? I know he would want to believe it was true, but honestly." She shook her head, and her perfect posture slumped.

"We're as certain as we can be, and we'll have definite proof tomorrow, but your husband is sure. He and Dax talked at length and reminisced about childhood memories. Dax knew things he simply couldn't have known if he hadn't been there."

Her eyes narrowed. "Why would he put Frank through all these years of suffering? That's simply unforgiveable. Frank hasn't ever been the same since he lost him. If it really is Dax, he has some explaining to do." With a harumph, she reached for her water again.

"In Dax's defense, he was young and scared. He was also convinced his dad had tried to kill him. You see, he left Frank a message on his office phone the day before. Frank says he never received the message, which means someone else in the office did."

She frowned. The pink in her cheeks faded. "Why on earth would he think Frank wanted to kill him? That is preposterous."

"Dax had spent the summer traveling with the division and was determined to get to the bottom of what caused the accidents. He was convinced someone at corporate was behind it. He uncovered evidence of falsifying maintenance logs and not replacing parts that should have been. Everything he learned led back to the corporate office. He called and told his dad that and revealed his location, and the next thing that happened was his RV exploded, and he was presumed dead. I think he was quite logical at the time."

Her eyes widened, and her lips quivered. "That can't be. Frank would never do such a thing."

Coop nodded. "I tend to agree with you. Now, I think Dax is convinced it wasn't his father, and Frank wants to help him get to the bottom of it. If it wasn't Frank, it had to be someone with access to Frank's office and that answering machine."

Adele's eyes widened. "Or the message could have simply not been recorded. Those machines aren't perfect, you know."

"That's another possibility. We'll be looking at all angles, trust me." Coop stood, and AB followed his lead. She placed one of their cards on the coffee table next to Adele's glass.

"We'll see ourselves out, Ms. Covington," said Coop. "If you think of anything that may help, please do give us a call. I'm sure we'll see you again once you're back in Nashville."

By the time they checked in next door, Coop was tired. They had adjoining rooms and while he contemplated a nap, he heard a tap on the connecting door.

He opened it to find AB decked out in her swimming suit. "I'm heading down to the beach. Do you want to join me?"

He sighed. "I'm exhausted and was just thinking about a nap."

"You can nap at the beach. Come on, get your trunks on and make the most of the few hours we have left here."

How could she be so energetic? He promised to meet her in the lobby in a few minutes.

He tugged on a white t-shirt lettered with FITNESS PROTECTION PROGRAM I'M HIDING FROM EXERCISE. He found and donned his sunglasses and grabbed his notebook and pen. When he got downstairs, AB already had a towel for him and had figured out the best place for them to enjoy the ocean view. She had arranged chairs for them on the beach and made a reservation for dinner at the casual restaurant where the hostess recommended a table that would afford them a sunset view.

Coop followed AB through the property and out to the white beach so unspoiled, it looked fake. They found their lounge chairs ready, iced teas on the table next to them, and an umbrella positioned to shade their faces, should they need it.

Coop rested against the warm chair and gazed out at the idyllic blue waters of the Gulf of Mexico and the tension in his back and shoulders eased. AB was already at the edge of the water, dipping her toes into it and waving at him. Thoughts of the case swirled in his mind, but he placed his notebook in the beach bag AB had lugged down with her and shut his eyes.

He needed to let all he had learned percolate, and there was no better place to relax than Clearwater Beach.

10

M onday morning dawned with a gorgeous blue sky and the bright sun peeking above the horizon. Coop made his way to the beach for an early morning walk. After his nap on the chaise lounge yesterday, AB had talked him into a swim in the lagoon-style pool before dinner.

He had made it an early night and like the last time he had taken a trip where he could hear the soft sound of the ocean waves at night, he slept soundly. Maybe he was destined to live near the coast, instead of landlocked Nashville.

He kept his phone in the pocket of his shorts, hoping he'd get an email from Janice with the DNA results. Once that was confirmed, he'd let Ben know so he could get the signature from Frank to allow for the exhumation, which would start another cold case for Ben and the authorities in Georgia. That would also draw the attention of the media. That was something that wouldn't be welcomed.

Walking the quiet beach as the sun rose was heavenly. With the cool sand beneath his feet, the soft slap of the waves on the shore, and the gorgeous colors of the sky and sea, Coop couldn't help but relax. The only thing that would have made it better was Gus by his side, but Coop was sure Camille and his dad would be spoiling him.

As he walked, he organized the next phase of the investigation, which would require tracking down the employees from Royal and Big Top to see what he could learn about Red Fulton. Huck was also high on the list of people he wanted to interview, and he wanted to probe Dax's memory for anyone who worked with him that summer who might be helpful.

Cases usually turned on a small bit of information that served as the key to unlock everything. Now, they just had to find that elusive key among all the people who worked at Royal who might know something—even something they didn't realize was important.

He turned around and made his way back to the resort, soaking in the beauty and beach vibes one last time before they had to leave for the airport. After a shower and slipping into a t-shirt decorated with a huge cup of coffee and lettered with SORRY FOR WHAT I SAID BEFORE I HAD MY COFFEE, Coop repacked his bag and met AB in the restaurant for breakfast.

He found her sitting at an outdoor table, staring at the water. They sipped fresh coffee and enjoyed the selection of pastries and fruit that would keep their hunger at bay while they navigated the airport and got back to Nashville. The waiter was nice enough to suggest he package the leftovers in takeaway containers for them to take on the plane.

Coop leaned back and sighed. "I could get used to this, but duty calls."

AB gathered her things. "Maybe we need a satellite office in Florida. If so, I call dibs on running it." She laughed, and they said goodbye to the beach and hello to their shuttle driver.

Airports, the lines, the entire process of airline travel made Coop's head hurt. He was cranky, and his tolerance was low. Years ago, it had been fun, almost a novelty when he was growing up, but now, it was a royal pain. He tried to use all the time waiting in lines and waiting for boarding and waiting for takeoff to focus on Dax's case instead of his impatience at the entire process.

Despite doing nothing, he was exhausted by the time AB dropped him off in front of the house. Adding to his frustration was the arrival of Janice's email while they were in the air, so he didn't see it until they landed. "See you in the morning, Coop," AB said with a wave.

Coop opened the door to the smiling face of Gus, and his spirits lifted. He grinned and rubbed Gus under his chin, feeling happier with each flick of the dog's tail against his legs. He heard Aunt Camille and his dad chattering in the kitchen and after depositing his overnight bag in his room, he put in a call to Dax to let him know the DNA results were conclusive. Frank and Dax were father and son, and now they had the legal proof.

He felt Dax's relief through the phone. "I'm going to call your dad now and let him know. The authorities will be in touch to begin the exhumation."

"He's prepared, I think. He'd just like to keep the matter as private as possible. Nobody needs the publicity and the whole story dug up again." He sucked in a breath, "Poor choice of words, sorry. We're hoping to avoid attention, especially as you're trying to figure out what actually happened. The more I talked to Dad, the more I'm convinced he never got my message and never knew anything about the falsified paperwork."

"That's good to hear. We'll be working on some leads this week, and I'll be in touch as soon as I know more."

Next, he rang Frank, technically his co-client, and shared the good news. Frank sighed. "I didn't believe it that first day at Lindsay's, but the minute I saw my son's eyes, and we talked, I knew it was him. I didn't need the fancy test, but it will help with everything else that will have to happen. I'd like to see you about my estate and changes I need to make to my will."

"I'm happy to help you with that. I'll have AB get in touch

when we're back in the office tomorrow and set something up right away."

"I appreciate that. The sooner, the better. It would put my mind at ease."

"Understood. We'll make it happen tomorrow."

Frank thanked him and added, "I spoke with Adele after your visit. She wanted to pass her apologies to you and AB. She was shocked at the news and feared she wasn't her normally hospitable self. She was quite upset with me that I hadn't told her about Dax."

"No need to apologize. We know the news is difficult, but it helps us to be able to get fresh reactions and memories from everyone. We'll be hitting that hard this week to try to contact everyone who worked in your office. We need to figure out who intercepted Dax's message to you."

"Or like Adele said, that blasted machine wasn't always reliable."

Coop didn't state the obvious. Frank didn't need more to worry about. Without someone listening to the message, the killer wouldn't have known where Dax was staying. If the fire was truly an accident, it didn't matter, but Coop had learned long ago not to believe in coincidences, and this one was too strong to ignore.

Coop disconnected and texted Ben the news he had been anticipating, asking that they conduct the exhumation as quietly as possible. With that done, he joined his dad and Camille in the kitchen.

"Oh, Coop, how was your trip?" said Camille, as he watched her pour the pecan icing over the still warm sheet cake on the counter. The rich, chocolate pecan cake was a favorite of his and his stomach rumbled with hunger. He couldn't wait to dig into it.

He sighed. "It was a good trip. I'm glad we talked to Mrs.

Covington, and you can't beat the winter weather in Florida, but I'm always happy to be home."

As they settled in for one of Aunt Camille's delicious suppers of pulled pork on homemade rolls, a crisp cabbage salad, and warm applesauce, she brought him up to date on the happenings at the office during his absence. Charlie let him know that Camille was still in the lead, but he was catching up to her, having won several games of Gin Rummy while they babysat the office. Coop was starving, having only eaten a small breakfast, and made quick work of his sandwich while he listened.

By the time Aunt Camille brought out her cake with the thick chocolate icing full of pecans, Coop was full but took a small piece, knowing she had gone to the trouble to make his favorites to welcome him home. They lingered as they enjoyed dessert, and Charlie and Camille wanted to know all about his impressions after interviewing Adele and Gavin.

"AB and I didn't like Gavin, and Adele was aloof, but nothing they said implicated them. We didn't tell Gavin about Dax but divulged that little morsel to Adele. She was shocked, to the say the least, and then seemed angry that Dax had let his dad suffer all these years by disappearing. She assured us that Frank would never do anything to harm Dax and thought it was preposterous for him to think so."

Coop took another bite of the sinful cake. "We did get a few more leads on other people who worked at Royal Amusement at the time of the accidents and the fire at Dax's trailer. AB and I will be following up on all of them to see if we can get anything concrete from any of them. Red Fulton's name came up, as he was the owner of Big Top, Frank's main competitor, and he'd been wanting to buy Royal for quite some time and eventually did, after Dax's death."

Camille nodded. "Sounds like motive right there."

Coop smirked. "Problem is, he's dead, so it makes him difficult to interview. We'll have to see if we can find anybody who's still around from those days at Big Top. These old cases are tough."

Camille reached for the pitcher of iced tea. "I've met Adele at a few charity events, and she's always been nice enough. She's always dressed to the nines, and we all think she's had lots of plastic surgery. We belong to several of the same clubs, but Adele doesn't do much, except write big checks. She strikes me as a little big for her britches and someone who doesn't like to get her hands dirty with real work."

"If you think she's bad, you should meet her son. He has zero empathy for Frank and almost laughed when he talked about him dying soon. AB and I thought he was slimy and a pompous jerk."

Camille shrugged. "I don't know him, and it sounds like I'm not missing much. Frank and Adele live down the road a spell and over the years, our paths have crossed at various events. He always strikes me as a kind man, much like his daughter. Lindsay's a real sweetheart. You'd never know they had money. Adele, though, she sort of flaunts it."

Coop finished his last bite and licked every speck of icing from his fork. "That's the impression we got yesterday. She was tolerant of us, offering us a drink, but was put out by our intrusion. In her defense, we did surprise her."

"Frank's first wife Laura Beth was a dear. Down to earth and quite lovely. It's a shame."

Coop stood and collected the dirty plates. "Thanks for holding down the fort and watching out for Gus. I'm glad the office wasn't very busy, and you had time to play cards. I'm going to call it a night and be at the office early in the morning to catch up."

After more sleep than usual, Coop and Gus were up while it was still dark and at the office before five in the morning. The chill in the air called for a fire and once he got one started, he brewed coffee and settled in at his desk while Gus hopped onto his chair and closed his eyes.

Coop tapped Bethany's name into the computer and scanned the results. Lewis was a common surname and returned several results, even when narrowing down the region. He captured a few possibilities, based on age and residential address twenty-five years ago.

Next, Coop tried Marvin Eastman. He had better luck and found the former salesman currently living thirty minutes away in Mt. Juliet. He added his address and phone number to his notebook. He noted that Marvin had indeed worked for Big Top when the business sold and was currently retired.

He noticed an email notification pop up and frowned when he saw Darcy Flint's name as the sender. She was his mother's lawyer in Vermont. The muscles in his shoulders tightened as he clicked on the message.

He read the short paragraph. Since he was paying the bill, Ms. Flint kept him informed, and she wanted to remind him that his mother would be released from jail next week but would need to fulfill her community service requirement. With her outbursts at the judge, he had tacked on the maximum, and it would take her another two weeks if she could get in eight hours of work per day.

Coop's temples throbbed. The shirt he wore today was appropriate—

YOU CALL THEM SWEAR WORDS, I PREFER SENTENCE ENHANCERS. He resisted the urge to

. . .

shout out several of them and pounded the keys on his keyboard in frustration.

With her tucked away in a jail cell more than a thousand miles away, he had relegated Marlene to the far recesses of his mind. Thinking about her only brought anguish, and he had taken his aunt and AB's advice and tried to forget about her and her nastygrams that she had taken to sending every few days.

AB hadn't given him any more of them, but he knew she culled the mail for them and hid the envelopes filled with venom before Coop saw them. His hopes of time away where his mother could reflect on her own actions and maybe take responsibility had faded the moment he read the first letter from her. Nothing was ever Marlene's fault. She hadn't changed since the day she walked out on Charlie more than twenty years ago.

Ms. Flint suggested a few inexpensive motels where Marlene could stay while she completed her community service. The lawyer had done her best to ask that the community service be transferred to another jurisdiction, since Marlene wasn't actually a resident of the tiny town where she had committed her crimes. She was only there visiting with her friend Ruben, who was also in jail. The judge was having none of it, especially with Marlene not having a stable history or home address. He insisted she complete her service before she left town.

Coop didn't blame him. His mom was a flake and a disgrace. With everyone he had seen from his perch on the bench, Coop was sure he saw what Marlene was and knew she couldn't be trusted. It had taken Coop much longer to accept that about her.

Ms. Flint had also supplied a list of a handful of community programs that typically took in community service workers. After a quick scan of the list, Coop shook his head. Marlene would be mortified to have to stoop to the level of picking up garbage, cleaning park restrooms, or washing dishes at the senior center. He was glad he wasn't the one who would break the news to her and said a little prayer for Ms. Flint.

He tapped in a reply and let her know he would cover the cost of the motel for up to three weeks after Marlene's release. That would give his mother time enough to get in her hours and motivate her to get it done in a timely manner. He suggested the lawyer add the cost to her bill, as he wouldn't agree to send Marlene the money directly, and asked Ms. Flint to coordinate with the motel. He thanked her for her time and patience and hit the send button.

One more week of quiet was all he had, and then maybe three weeks before she'd be back, looking for a handout or be in trouble again. He could only hope she and Ruben would ride off into the sunset and live happily ever after. Sadly, they had a better chance of sharing a jail cell somewhere.

Gus darted across the office and to the back door. Moments later, Coop was surprised to hear Ben's voice talking to Gus as he came down the hallway. His old friend smiled and held up a bag from Epic Bagels. Ben had a serious addiction to the new shop that opened a few months ago. "Thought I'd stop by with a treat for you and AB and update you on the plan."

"If your plan requires a bagel bribe, I'm not sure I'm going to like it." Coop hurried to the kitchen and grabbed some plates and utensils.

As they added schmears of cream cheese and jam to their selections, Ben explained, "We'll have no problem getting an order of exhumation, based on the DNA results. We're going to work with the cemetery and keep a low profile. Thought we could cordon off the section where the grave is and try to sell it as a routine maintenance project. The funeral home director agreed to wear a construction vest, and I'll do the same. We'll keep it as low profile as possible and transfer the casket to the medical examiner's office, and they'll fill in the hole. We'll try to get it done quickly, late in the day."

Coop took a long swallow from his mug, letting the rich coffee warm his throat and soothe his soul. The dark elixir and the fresh bagel helped him forget about his mother and focus on the case at hand.

Coop added a bit more cream cheese to his cinnamon raisin bagel. "That sounds good and about all you can do to limit the curiosity. The story will get out soon enough, I think the Covington family is hoping to keep it from becoming a spectacle."

Ben nodded as he slipped the last bite of his cheese bagel in his mouth. "Georgia isn't interested in shining the light on their original screw up. Not that I blame them. Nobody would have gone to the trouble and expense of a forensic dental exam back then, especially with nobody to compare it to and no question on identity. It's just embarrassing for them."

Coop's head bobbed. "I get it, but Nate's family deserves to know what happened to him. I'm just hoping you can find out who he is."

Ben brushed the crumbs from his tie and stood. "We've agreed to help, since we have more resources. I'll keep you posted, and we're shooting for Thursday for the exhumation."

"I'm going to try to find some of their original witnesses from the carnival. Thanks for the bagels. I'll be sure to save one for AB."

"I'll get one of the detectives to see if they can find anything current on the witness list and shoot it over if we have any luck."

"That would be great. I've got to find time to squeeze Frank Covington in today. He wants to discuss his will and needs help with his estate."

Ben's eyes rose. "That should be interesting." He grabbed a

napkin from the table. "I gotta run. See you Friday for breakfast if not before."

Gus got a quick rub behind the ears on Ben's way out the door. Coop followed him to the kitchen where he polished off the last bit of real coffee in the pot. While Gus stared out the window at the back door, watching Ben leave, AB pulled into the parking lot, and his tail wagged in quick arcs.

She greeted him with her sweet voice and a thorough neck rub before setting a pot of decaf to brew. "Morning, AB," Coop said, as he meandered out of the kitchen. He listened to her talk to Gus while she turned on her computer. A few minutes later, AB came through the door, with Gus following her. Coop offered her a bagel, courtesy of Ben.

As she ate breakfast, Coop checked his notepad. "Go ahead and get Frank in here first thing, and that will put his mind at ease. I want to visit Marvin in Mt. Juliet. I'll probably leave here early and head over there late this afternoon. I want to surprise him, like we did Gavin and Adele." He filled her in on Ben's news about the exhumation and his offer to help locate the witnesses from the carnival.

She jotted a note on her notepad. "Got it." After she finished her bagel, she took her cup and stood.

"One more thing, I agreed to pay for three weeks at a motel for Marlene. Ms. Flint will add it to the bill. She's got to do her community service after she gets out of jail next week."

He didn't ask about any more letters from his mother, and AB didn't volunteer any information before taking her notebook and heading to her desk. Marlene was usually a topic best left unsaid.

11

F rank arrived, along with Lindsay and Dax, before noon.
AB reminded him to change his shirt and with a fresh
button down, Coop welcomed them into his office, and AB left
them with a tray of hot coffee, tea, and cookies.

Frank, dressed in a jacket and tie, cleared his throat and
glanced at Lindsay and Dax before turning to Coop. "Thanks
for seeing us so quickly. As you know, I'm unwell and don't
know how much time I have." His eyes glistened and met Dax's.
"Not nearly enough, I'm afraid. I want to make sure my estate
goes to Lindsay and Dax. Adele and I have a prenuptial agreement. I've made provisions for Adele and will keep those, of
course, but Dax's appearance has changed some things. I want
Dax and Lindsay in charge of the company. Previously, I had
put Gavin in that role, but like Adele, I'd rather make a provision for him and leave everything to my children. They can
make the best decisions on how to proceed in the future,
together. I want my legacy to be in my family's hands."

He pulled an envelope from his inner jacket pocket and slid
it across the table. "You'll find a copy of my old will and all the
pertinent estate information there. I couldn't find the prenuptial

agreement, but the law office retained a copy." He mentioned an attorney who had died a few years ago, but Coop recognized him from law school and as an original partner of one of the big firms downtown. "I've told them you'll be handing the revisions and instructed them to provide anything you need."

Coop scanned the documents and the sticky note Frank had attached listing out the amount of money that would go to Gavin. "This is a relatively simple change. Are you sure you wouldn't rather just have the existing firm handle it for you? I don't think it would take them long."

Frank grinned. "An honest attorney. You're like a rare species, you know that, son?" He chuckled and smiled. "I'd rather have you handle it here. You've got a small office, and that firm downtown is filled with people. Some of whom I'm sure would like nothing more than to wag their tongues about my affairs. I trust you." He looked between his children. "We trust you, and that's what's important."

Coop nodded. "I appreciate your confidence. We'll get right on this and have the new documents drawn up this week." Coop took a sip from his cup. "I talked with the police this morning about the exhumation, and they're keeping it as quiet as possible, framing it as some routine maintenance, but they will have it completed by Thursday. No guarantees, of course, that it won't be noticed."

Frank nodded. "I understand. I'll be prepared in case the press gets wind of it."

Coop put the envelope aside and slid his notebook in front of him. "Have any of you had any more ideas about who might have been behind the fire? Red Fulton is near the top of my list, but he's deceased, and it's not likely anyone at the company now will know much. I'm planning to see Marvin Eastman today and still haven't made contact with Huck Grover yet but hoping they can shed some light on it."

Dax cleared his throat. "In my mind, it had to be someone in

Dad's office. Like you say, maybe they were working for Red Fulton, but it boils down to someone who had access to my message."

Coop tapped his pen on the pad. "I agree. That's why we're anxious to talk to everyone who worked there." He turned his eyes toward Frank. "Do you remember if anyone was absent from work the day of the fire?"

Frank's eyes widened. "Oh, my, that's asking quite a bit from this old brain. I don't remember much about that day except for the horrific news about Dax. I was dumbfounded, and it didn't make any sense to me at first."

Coop moved the pen down his notepad. "The carnival boss, Rex Fitch, is also deceased. I was hoping he might have more information. I'm reviewing the witness list the Georgia police spoke with and am working on locating them."

Dax drummed his fingers on the table. "Rex was a pretty good guy. Gruff and always busy. Most of the evidence I collected came from his office. Not really an office, per se, but he kept a notebook and always wrote down his conversations and had several things recorded in there about receiving directions from HQ, what he always called the corporate office, directing the carnival bosses to cut back on maintenance to boost profits. Dad and I have talked about this at length and if it didn't come from him, it had to come from someone in authority, like Huck or Marvin. Someone who could speak for Dad and get away with it."

Coop frowned. "If you didn't know anything about this or direct it, Frank, it does seem like it was someone working against you from the inside. Maybe someone helping make sure Red Fulton could acquire the company at a steal of a price."

Frank sighed and shook his head. "I can't imagine Red would stoop so low, but sadly, anything is possible. He did end up getting the company for a lower price than I would have liked. Much of it due to the accidents, and some of it was due to the grief I was under at losing Laura Beth and Dax. I just didn't care anymore."

Lindsay and Dax both reached a hand to comfort their father. He looked down at the table. "All I know is whoever is responsible, robbed me of far too many years with my son. Dax is convinced it wasn't an accident and while I wish he would have trusted me, I understand him running away to protect himself."

Tears filled Dax's eyes as he patted his father's arm. "Like I told you before, Coop, there was nothing wrong with the RV. I used the water heater each day and never had a problem with the pilot light. It wasn't windy, and I'm convinced someone tampered with it, causing the interior to fill with propane. All it would take is a spark. Like from a cigarette. Nate smoked, and I left him with my pack of cigarettes. I only smoked to fit in and learn as much as possible from the workers who gathered for smoke breaks. Deep down, I know it wasn't a fluke or an accident."

Coop put his pen down. "I agree with you, Dax. It's just too much of a coincidence and could easily be mistaken for an accident. The problem is physical evidence from twenty-five years ago is gone. Nobody looked at foul play, so the accident was a plausible conclusion."

Dax hung his head. "I should have called or something long ago. It's hard to explain, but it was easier to ignore and just immerse myself in my fake life. It hurt too much to think about the past."

Lindsay dabbed at her eyes. "We're just glad to have you back, Dax. That's what matters most." She glanced at her father. "Let's get some lunch, Dad. Then, we'll get you home to rest."

The stress of the situation showed in Frank's sunken cheeks and tired eyes. He leaned against Dax as he stood and extended his hand to Coop. "Thank you for helping us, and I pray you get to the bottom of it."

"I'll do my best, sir. We'll be in touch as soon as we have the new documents ready for your signature."

Coop saw them out, handed AB the estate documents, and then sunk into the couch in the reception area, not far from AB's desk. "Shift the will and estate to the top priority. Frank is worried and wants to button everything up before he gets any worse."

"I'll get right on it. It's so sad to know they missed out on all those years, and now he doesn't have much time left."

The utter heartbreak between Dax and his family was easy to see and hard to watch. It wasn't fair and bolstered Coop's resolve to get to the bottom of it all. After signing off on a couple of files in his office and a quick bite to eat, he patted Gus on the head. "You stay here with AB, and she'll make sure you get home tonight, buddy."

Gus was always up for an outing, but with AB being one of his favorite humans, he didn't object and curled into a spot he favored near the edge of her desk.

"Wish me luck, AB. If I'm not back by closing, just drop Gus off at the house."

Coop made it to Mt. Juliet in under an hour and drove by Marvin's tidy brick home in the quiet neighborhood not far from the banks of the Cumberland River. There was an older sedan in the driveway, which Coop took as a good sign that the owner was home. He parked down the street and punched in Marvin's phone number.

After a few rings, a man answered and after Coop inquired, he learned it was Marvin. Coop explained he was investigating an old case related to Royal Amusement and Frank Covington, and Marvin agreed to an impromptu visit. Coop disconnected and waited ten minutes before he started the Jeep and parked at the curb.

A lanky man with a shiny bald head, ringed in long gray hair answered Coop's knock. The silvery and white strands weren't just past his collar, they hung to the middle of Marvin's back. He welcomed Coop with a friendly smile and led him into the cozy living room.

Coop noted the guitar resting in the corner as he took a seat. Marvin pointed at a cup of coffee on the side table next to his chair. "Can I get you a cup?"

Coop shook his head. "Thanks, but I'm fine."

Marvin nodded and sat. "You said you're looking into something for Frank Covington?"

"Right. It's actually going back twenty-five years to when his son was killed in the fire at the carnival site in Georgia. I understand you were working at Royal at the time and had been for several years."

"Oh, yes, that was awful. Poor Frank. He had lost his wife a few months before that. It was a horrible time, really."

Coop asked many of the same questions he had asked of Adele and Gavin. Marvin's recollection matched up with theirs, including the open access to Frank's office. Coop listened as Marvin explained most of his workday consisted of talking on the phone and organizing bookings for the carnival all over the United States.

"Am I correct that you went to work for Big Top after they bought Royal?"

Marvin nodded and rolled his eyes. "Yes, for a short time. I wasn't thrilled about moving to Ohio, but at the time, didn't have many options. Let's just say I became more motivated and ended up leaving after about a year. Eventually, I got back here to the Nashville area and did bookings for musicians. That was where my heart was all along. I think I had locked myself into thinking all I could sell was carnivals, and it took the jolt of moving and working in a place I didn't like to spur me into action."

Coop scribbled a note. "Do you think Red could have been behind the accidents at Royal's carnival sites? It was common knowledge that Red wanted to buy Royal, so maybe he thought he could get a better price or force Frank to sell?"

His brows arched. "Wow, I honestly don't know. I wouldn't have thought anyone would take such extreme steps, but who knows? Frank ran Royal more like a family. We had a small group at the corporate office, and I think we all worked hard and enjoyed it there, but Big Top was another story. I never interacted with Red much. I was just a cog in the wheel."

"From what I understand, part of the sales agreement included providing jobs to everyone who worked in the field and many of those in the corporate office. Did your assistant Penny also take a position at Big Top? And do you know her last name?"

Marvin chuckled. "Penny Robbins was and is her name. And no, she was smarter than I was. She didn't want to uproot her family and move. She found a job working at a school and still lives in the area."

Coop wrote down her name and contact information. "What about Bethany Lewis, do you know where she might be now?"

"Oh, she was in payroll, and she also didn't make the transition to Big Top. I know she ended up divorced. Penny could probably tell you more. She was close to Bethany and Alice, who was an assistant in the payroll office. They were more plugged into the office chatter and spent time together outside of work."

"Was there anyone you worked with at Royal who might have held a grudge against Frank or could have been involved in creating those accidents, maybe helping Red?"

His clear-blue eyes widened. "Again, I never considered that." He frowned as he thought. "Everyone seemed happy and worked together quite well. The only hiccup was when Gavin came on board. I don't think he and Huck got along, and Gavin was, well, arrogant and young. Full of himself."

Coop nodded, thinking Gavin hadn't changed much. "You mentioned Huck. I've been trying to get in touch with him and left a couple of messages, but I haven't heard back. Are you still in contact with him?"

"I know he lives in Brentwood. I ran into him, oh, I guess it was last year. We chatted, but I'm not close to him. I know he left before the sale was finalized and took a job in Memphis."

"Did that surprise you?"

Marvin's forehead creased. "Yeah, a little. He had been with Frank from the beginning. Maybe he saw the writing on the wall and wanted to get out while he could. He was smarter than I was, too. Red followed the agreement and offered everyone a job, but it wasn't like what we were used to at Royal. I always felt Frank valued my opinions, but it wasn't the same with Red. I hated going to work and kicked myself for moving and then having to start over when I moved back here."

"What about Dax's death in the fire? Do you have any insight or theories on that?"

He hung his head, and his shoulders drooped. "That was a horrible day. Just awful. I felt so bad for Frank. He was still reeling from the loss of Laura Beth, who by the way was a sweetheart of a woman. Dax was a nice young man. I wasn't close or involved with their family, but I know Frank was shocked to learn Dax had been down in Georgia traveling with Rex's crew. It was such a blow to the poor man. He was never the same after that."

Coop asked if Marvin remembered anyone being absent from work that day. Marvin shook his head. "I couldn't tell you. I remember working that day, and I know Penny was there, but we were in our own little bubble most of the time. I don't know about anyone else in the office."

"Was there ever a hint that it might not have been an accident?"

Marvin sat back in the chair and sighed. "Boy, not that I ever heard. Everything pointed to an accident, something with a faulty pilot light, if memory serves. Are you saying it wasn't an accident?"

"Frank hired us to look into it. There is some new information in the case, and he's not convinced it was an accident. Same with the supposed accidents at the carnival sites. Did you ever hear anything through the grapevine about falsified maintenance records on the equipment?"

Marvin's eyes narrowed. "No, never. Frank wouldn't stand for that. Royal had a great reputation for maintenance. That was a priority. The business office kept meticulous records on all the equipment at each site. I know there was a long investigation into it and from what I recall, Royal's insurance paid out huge sums to those poor families. They went through our records with a fine-toothed comb. I never heard an inkling of that idea."

Coop closed the cover on his notebook. "All of it does seem to benefit Big Top and Red Fulton, doesn't it? The accidents, the press coverage, the insurance payout, and the subsequent agreement from Frank to sell after so many years of resisting. All that together with the loss of his wife and then Dax's death, it just seems like more than bad luck."

Marvin took another sip from his cup and studied Coop. "When you put it like that, I can see what you mean. All I can tell you is it never crossed my mind, and I never heard any gossip about it. We were all devastated for Frank and the company. I know Frank is very ill, and I'm sure he's struggling. I should make time to see him. Before it's too late."

"I'm sure he'd appreciate that." Coop stood and handed Marvin his business card. "You've been very helpful. If you think of anything further, especially related to the accidents or the fire in Georgia, please call me."

Marvin stood and shook Coop's hand. "It's been a long time, but I'll think more on it." He walked Coop to the door. "Be sure to tell Frank hello for me, and I'll call on him soon."

Coop thanked him and headed to the Jeep. He keyed in the phone number for Penny Robbins and left a message when her voicemail greeted him. It was close to quitting time, and he needed to let what Marvin told him marinate a bit. He drove back to the highway and steered the Jeep to the office, intent on picking up Gus and taking him for a walk in the park before heading home.

Gus would love the romp and walking outside always helped Coop think better. Marvin struck him as an honest guy. His gut told him Marvin wasn't involved in anything sinister, but he needed to think about all the details. He hoped the distraction would lodge something loose and lead him to the key to solving this one.

12

The next morning, AB rang through to Coop's office with Penny Robbins on the line, returning his call. He spoke to her for a few minutes and set up a time to meet at a coffee shop near to the office when she had her lunch break. He asked her if she happened to know how to get in touch with Bethany Lewis, and Penny let him know she was now Bethany Hooper, and she also worked in the school district. Penny offered to contact her and have her join them if Bethany could make it work.

Coop updated Bethany's information and rewarded himself for checking two people off the list by finishing off the last of his fully caffeinated coffee, which he wished he would have warmed before swallowing.

AB was busy working the phone, following up on the original witnesses at the site of the fire. Ben had provided current information on them, and none of them were local, so it would take some time online and over the phone. Coop wanted to interview them via video, since body language and facial expressions were often more telling than words.

Coop sat on the couch petting Gus while she finished her call. When she hung up, he said, "Can you get in touch with

Judge Monroe's office today and see if he can squeeze me in for a hearing, so we can bring Dax back to life legally. I'll need the death certificate rescinded and want it done as soon as possible and a matter of record. You can put together the information from the DNA analysis, the law enforcement reports, and the order of exhumation for me, and I'll make it work whenever he can get me in for a quick hearing."

AB scribbled a note on her pad. "I'll get it put together and call this morning." She frowned at the shirt he was wearing—I'M JUST HERE TO ESTABLISH AN ALIBI.

He glanced down at it and zipped up his jacket. "There, that works. I promise to keep it covered." She rolled her eyes and went back to her work.

Coop set out for the Mainline Coffee and ordered a decaf mocha. He couldn't resist the friendly smile of the woman named Liz behind the counter who offered him a free cinnamon roll, which he also found to be irresistible. With it being eleven o'clock and the morning rush over, he had his choice of tables and selected one in the corner with a good view of the entrance.

He'd eaten half of the pastry and taken his first sip when he noticed two women, both of whom wore lanyards with school identification badges, come through the door. He made eye contact with the strawberry blonde and brunette and said, "You must be Penny and Bethany?"

They smiled and nodded. He led the way to the counter. "My treat, ladies." The barista wasn't quite as friendly during his second visit, and no free pastry offers were extended as he explained he was paying for the women's lunch.

They ordered coffees and salads and after he paid, they waited for their orders and joined him at the table. "Thanks so much for meeting me today." He focused on Bethany, with heavy silver strands in her dark hair. He guessed her to be in her mid-fifties. "I'm Cooper Harrington, and as Penny probably explained, I'm looking into an old case for Frank Covington."

He went through his litany of questions, and they confirmed Frank's office was accessible to all, but as Marvin had suspected, they were more tuned into the office gossip than he had been. Bethany reiterated what others had shared about Huck and Gavin. "Huck was a great boss, serious about work, but always friendly. That all changed after Gavin started working in our department. He acted as if he didn't have to work very hard because of his mom Adele. Not everyone caught on as she went by Adele West, and his last name was Pierce. It didn't take long for him to make it known she was his mom. It was awkward to say the least."

Coop consulted his notebook. "Did Gavin do a good job? What was your impression?"

Bethany's forehead wrinkled. "He had the education and knew all processes but had no respect for Huck. He was a know-it-all and came off as arrogant. He was the youngest one there and thought he should be in charge. I felt sorry for Huck. He did his best to tolerate Gavin and tried to channel him in the right direction, but Gavin had a habit of circumventing Huck and going through his mom to Frank. Huck grew tired of it and looked for a job before Frank decided to sell."

Coop penned a note. "Frank is convinced there is more to the accidents at the carnival sites. Do either of you have any thoughts about someone working in the office who could have been trying to sabotage Royal? Maybe someone working with Red Fulton, who wanted to buy Frank out?"

Penny, her brows raised above her pale blue eyes, glanced at Bethany. After a tiny nod from the dark-haired woman, she turned her attention to Coop. "I'm sure it's nothing, but one night in December, I remember because of all the decorations, I went for drinks with a friend at the Oak Bar downtown at the

Hermitage Hotel. It's not a place I would normally go, but she was in town for business and was staying there."

She took a long swallow from her cup. "I saw Adele and Red there. He had been in the office to meet with Frank earlier in the week. I thought it odd at the time, as I knew Red was trying to buy the business, and Adele was always so loyal to Frank, it didn't make sense."

Coop jotted on his notepad. "And this was December before the accidents that happened in the spring?" She nodded.

"Did they see you?"

Penny shook her head. "Oh, no. They were off to the side, and we were clear across the room. They were still there when we left for dinner, looking rather cozy. I mentioned it to Bethany, and we just wrote it off to Adele being Adele. We always got the impression she was looking for a rich guy, and this will sound bad, but she always struck me as wanting to be more than just Frank's secretary. Then, when his wife died, and they married so quickly, it made us wonder."

Coop sat back in his chair. "So, you think they were having an affair before Laura Beth died?"

Penny's jaw tightened, and she shrugged. "I never saw Frank behave unprofessionally. It's just a feeling, a vibe we got that Adele was looking for more. Like a purring cat rubbing up against him."

Bethany nodded. "She was one of those charming, petite women who liked to play dumb and innocent when it benefited her. She put herself above all of us, like she was something special because she was Frank's secretary. Underneath the cute blond hair and sweet face, I think she was cunning."

Penny stabbed a forkful of salad. "After Frank lost his wife, she swooped right in, doting on him and Lindsay. It didn't come as much of a surprise when they announced they were marrying."

Bethany snickered. "The only thing that shocked us was that

they went ahead with it so soon after Dax's death. It was so tragic, and Frank was like an empty man, just going through the motions of life. I'm not even sure he realized what was happening. We all felt so bad for him."

Coop nodded. "I can't imagine two such profound losses like that. You mentioned Dax. Tell me what you remember about that day at work. Was anyone absent that day? How did everyone react?"

Bethany shook her head. "I read about it in the paper the next morning. It happened after we had all left work. I remember walking into work that morning, trying to figure out what to say to Frank when I saw him. Everyone felt horrible, and we were all in shock. Nobody knew Dax had joined up to work with Rex's division. It was unbelievable."

Penny nodded. "We were all just sick. Everyone organized meals to take to Frank's house, and we were all worried about him and poor little Lindsay. That's too much to bear."

"Think back to that morning and the day before, if you will," said Coop, tapping his pen on his notepad. "Was anybody missing from work?"

Their foreheads creased as they thought. After a few minutes, Bethany spoke, "I know Huck was there and all the clerks in our office were there, because I remember going around with the sign-up sheet for food. I don't think Gavin was at work, only because I remember going by his office and thinking it was no great loss, since he couldn't be counted on for a meal anyway. I think he was out on the road, visiting a few sites. Huck sent him out sometimes to review the cash procedures and recordkeeping at the admission gate. Sort of like a surprise inspection." She laughed and added, "I think he did that mostly to get Gavin out of his hair."

Penny smiled. "I know Marvin was there. He was married at the time and said he and his wife would deliver a meal to the family. Adele was there for sure, flitting in and out, acting like she was standing in for Frank, when in reality, we all did our jobs and kept doing them. Frank took a few days off at home, so he wasn't there that next day. He came back after the funeral."

"Was there ever any mention that the fire that killed Dax wasn't an accident?"

They both gasped. Bethany shook her head. "Oh my gosh. Are you saying someone killed Dax?"

Coop kept his eyes focused on the pair. "I'm not saying anything, just asking questions."

"Poor Frank," said Penny as she continued to stare wide eyed.

Bethany took a sip of her coffee and then shook her head. "I never heard anything like that about the fire. I didn't know Frank suspected such a thing. We were all just sickened that he had to suffer another loss, and he loved Dax so much."

Coop thumbed the edge of his notepad. "Going back to Adele. Did anyone see her with Red at any other time? Was she involved in the negotiation of the sale of Royal at all?"

Penny shook her head. "I only saw her that one time, which is why I felt odd even saying anything. It was probably just a friendly holiday drink or something innocent."

Bethany let out a sigh. "I know Frank was involved in the negotiation of the sale. Huck had left by that point, and Gavin helped, but honestly, it wasn't much of a negotiation. Frank wanted out, and Red was in the wings waiting. From what I recall, we put together some information from the balance sheets and cash flows, and Red reviewed it and made an offer. I know it was lower than what we thought it should be, but Frank didn't squabble."

Coop nodded and turned to Penny. "So, based on Bethany's recollection that Frank was involved in the agreement, and it wasn't led by Adele, do you think she was colluding with Red to help him buy the company? I'm just trying to get to the heart of the matter and see if that's plausible."

Penny gritted her teeth. "I honestly don't know. I wouldn't think that one meeting at the bar would indicate collusion."

Bethany shook her head. "She wasn't overly involved in the sale. Just a go-between if we needed to provide documents to Frank, and he wasn't in the office. Gavin was the person who interfaced most with Frank. The clerks and I just prepared reports. Of course, Frank's lawyer was involved."

Coop glanced at his notes. "Do either of you know more about Alice, who worked there with you, I think, Bethany? Her last name and where she is now?"

Bethany put her cup down. "Alice was a sweet young woman, just out of high school, and it was her first job." She plucked her phone from her purse and scrolled through it. "She's married now, and her name is Alice Bartlett. She lives in Texas, but I've got her phone number." She recited it to Coop. "I don't see her often, but we stay in touch through Christmas cards. You should ask her about Gavin."

Coop finished adding the number to his notepad. "Right, okay. I think I've got it. I appreciate you both taking the time to talk to me." Coop passed each of them his card. "If you remember anything else or think something might be important, no matter how small, please call me."

He reached for his cup and stood. Bethany pointed at it and grinned. "Looks like you have an admirer. The barista gave you her phone number on your cup."

Coop turned it around and sure enough, Liz had added a phone number and her name with a little heart drawn above it. He shook his head. "I didn't even notice it."

He made for the door, hoping to avoid eye contact with Liz. He wondered how often her pickup method worked. He loved coffee, but he wasn't in the market for a date with a barista, especially one who he surmised was more than a decade younger. He'd learned his lesson last year with Shelby.

13

When Coop got back to the office, AB had organized video calls with two witnesses from the original police reports in Georgia. She hadn't had any luck finding the others yet. Both of them were set up for later in the afternoon, so Coop had time for a quick bite of lunch.

Aunt Camille had dropped off some soup and fresh bread while he had been meeting with Penny and Bethany. Coop helped himself to a bowl of the chicken and rice soup and a chunk of bread while he perused his notes from the meeting. He circled the reference to Gavin not being at work the day after the fire.

When he finished in the kitchen, he passed by AB's desk. She held up Frank's estate file. "I'll have this done today. If you have time to review it tomorrow, I'll schedule him to come in on Friday and sign the paperwork."

Coop nodded. "Great, I'll make sure to make it happen. I know he's worried, so go ahead and call him. That will make him feel better. I should have news on the exhumation by then, too."

He gave AB the note on Alice and asked her to set up

another video call with her, as soon as possible. While he waited for his first video interview, he put in a call to Dalton Jennings, Frank's lawyer, who had taken over the account for his father, Alistair Jennings when he died several years ago. He waited only a few minutes before Dalton came on the line.

"Mr. Harrington, Frank let us know you might be calling. How can I help?"

"I know it's a long shot, but I'm curious if you have any records from when your dad helped negotiate the sale of Royal Amusement twenty-five years ago? I'm digging into the old accidents that plagued the company and thought you might have some files I could look through. With your dad gone, I wasn't sure there would be anyone to talk to that might remember, so I figure the files are my best option."

The sound of keyboard keys clicking came through the phone. Moments later, Dalton said, "All I'm pulling up in our files right now that old is the prenuptial agreement Dad did for Frank's marriage to Adele."

"That's something I'll also need. Could you email that to my office?"

"Sure and let me do some digging. Dad would have been a great resource, and I don't know that he had anyone assisting him on that. He kept meticulous notes and records with all his files, so provided we still have them, they would be your best bet. I'm afraid everyone from Dad's era is gone. I'll look into it and get anything we have pulled together for you and sent to your office. Will that work?"

Coop thanked him and hung up the phone, staring at Gus, who was flopped across the leather chair, his legs in the air, and his mouth partially open, so his pink tongue flopped out of the side while he slept. Coop envied his ability to totally relax and sleep anywhere.

∾

After a look at the background AB had found on the first interviewee, Buster Riggs, Coop connected the video call. Buster was a young carny at the time of the incident, and he had been at the scene of the fire and had used the phone to call 911.

Moments later, the screen was filled with the face of a man Coop knew was close to his age, but the deep wrinkles in his face, heavy bags under his eyes, and sunken cheeks made him appear older. Buster had been a laborer at the carnival who also sometimes ran some of the games where patrons would toss coins or throw balls to win prizes. Currently, he was working at a tire shop in Nebraska.

Coop explained he was looking into the fire. "You were one of the first on the scene. Did you happen to see anyone hanging around the site that day? Someone who was new or didn't belong?"

Buster shook his head. "No, I was just walking that way and saw the explosion. Thank goodness I wasn't close to it. I ran up there, hoping Johnny wasn't inside, but when I didn't see him anywhere around the place, I sort of knew. It was horrific." Buster sighed. "Then we all heard that Johnny was Frank Covington's son and couldn't believe it."

Coop listened to him and then asked, "There's some new evidence that suggests the fire was deliberate. Can you think of anyone who might have had a grudge or could have known Johnny was Dax Covington?"

Buster shook his head. "Wow, that's horrible. We all just assumed it was an accident. Something with the pilot light. Johnny, uh, I guess Dax, smoked, so when the word came down about it being related to a propane leak causing the explosion, it made some sense. It was a real blow to everyone. We all liked him. He was a nice kid. Everyone was shocked he was a Covington. I remember Rex being beside himself over it all. He had no idea. I never ran across anybody who suspected Johnny was anybody other than Johnny."

Coop quizzed him more about the movements of people who worked at the carnival site and the workers who had trailers close to Dax's. From the photos and sketches included in the investigation files, it looked like Dax's trailer wasn't in the midst of the others and had been parked off to the side away from the other tents and trailers. Fortuitously, for all of them. It also meant someone could have slipped into the RV unnoticed and tampered with the propane.

Buster didn't have much to add but agreed it would be relatively easy to snuff out the pilot light and let the RV fill with propane. He shook his head and added, "I hope you find whoever did it. I know everybody judges carnies and thinks we're lowlifes, but I'm sure nobody who worked there would have done that."

Coop tapped his pen against his notebook. "Do you remember if anybody who was working there took off after the fire? Did anyone quit the carnival right after that day?"

Buster frowned. "Man, that was a long time ago. Casual laborers drifted in and out, so it wasn't something that would draw any attention. I guess it's possible, but nobody comes to mind. We were all pretty shook up about it, so I think someone would have said something if anybody just disappeared."

Coop nodded. "Are you still in touch with anyone from those days? Is there anybody you can think of that worked there that I should talk to that might be a source of information?"

Buster shook his head. "Nah, I didn't stay long after Frank sold the place. It was never the same when we got eaten up by Big Top. Rex would be the only one I could suggest, but he'd be fairly old by now, and I have no idea where he is."

Coop let him know Rex had passed away and thanked him for his time. Before Coop disconnected the video, he gave Buster his contact information and told him if he thought of anything to call him.

Coop had time for a cookie break before he had to interview

Dale Pressman. While he chewed on one of Aunt Camille's cookies, he wandered out to AB's desk. She handed him Frank's estate file with a smile. "All done and ready for you to review. He's coming in Friday at eleven o'clock. Frank's quite the honorable man. Despite their prenuptial agreement, he's been quite generous with Adele and Gavin."

"Yeah, they don't make them like Frank anymore. I'll take a look at this tonight. Could you contact Big Top and see if they happen to have any employment records from the time they took over Royal Amusement? I know it's a longshot, but I'd kick myself if I didn't at least try. It will make our witness list huge, but it might help us find someone who knows something about that day of the fire."

AB nodded and said, "I'm on it."

Coop took Frank's file and wandered back to his office, where Gus was still sleeping but did manage to pry open one eye to make sure there wasn't a dog treat in the cards before closing it again.

Coop perused the file on Dale Pressman, who had caught his eye because he had worked on the Swing-n-Shake, one of the more dangerous rides that had been involved in the deadly accident at another carnival site. He was a mechanic now, owned his own auto repair shop, and lived in Utah. From looking at his file, he hadn't stayed around to work for Big Top and instead took a job at an auto repair shop in rural Kentucky, where he had grown up and had family.

Coop connected the call and introduced himself to Dale, who was still dressed in his blue mechanic shirt with his name embroidered on a patch above his chest pocket. Dale was balding and from consulting his file, Coop saw he was fifty years old.

Coop ran through the basic questions he had asked everyone and when he mentioned the accidents and the idea of falsifying maintenance records, Dale nodded. "That's interesting because maintenance had always been a big deal at Royal. It was drilled into us to check and double check and when in doubt, replace any worn parts. Things shifted a little right before those accidents. Rex was frustrated. He said there was some double-talk coming out of HQ, which would be the corporate office in Nashville. He didn't say much but told me they were tightening the belt and wanted us to not waste money on unnecessary parts and maintenance. They wanted to get all the life they could out of everything. Rex and I both agreed we needed to keep on doing what we had been doing and keep things in the best shape. Maintenance is the key to making sure things lasted, so it didn't make much sense to be skimping, but Rex was tired of arguing. He dug into his own pocket or sometimes just skimmed the cash off the concessions to make sure we could buy whatever parts we needed."

Coop scribbled in his notebook. "So, were you ever told to falsify the maintenance records?"

Dale grimaced. "Rex said he was told to just check off the normal maintenance on our logs, but that his bonus would be tied to keeping those costs low. So, not in so many words, and Rex refused anyway. He wanted all the maintenance done as usual. We just couldn't show we were spending money on maintenance." Dale chuckled. "I think he liked the idea of pulling one over on the bean counters. He always said they thought they were so smart, and we were just a bunch of uneducated workers. If we had a big night, he'd buy a bunch of spare parts that we always used. He couldn't do that with the tickets themselves, since there was more of a strict accounting with them, but the concessions were all cash, and there was no real way he could get caught. He'd been doing it long enough, he knew how to keep the amount spent per person in line with the average. He was a smart guy. A nice guy. A good guy."

Coop added more notes. "Did Rex ever divulge who was telling him to cut back on maintenance? Was it Frank?"

Dale shook his head. "He never said. He actually never said much about HQ. This was some new directive that came about and then when those accidents happened, Rex was even more adamant that we just keep doing what we had been and maintaining things correctly. We were the biggest division and had the most chance of an accident, and he didn't want that to happen on his watch."

Coop nodded. "Did Rex involve anyone else in his scheme to keep maintaining things as usual and sort of divert money from one hand to feed the other?"

Dale shrugged "I don't think so. Rex trusted me, and I was good at fixing things, even back then. I supervised the maintenance on all the big rides and never said a word to anyone. Nothing changed as far as my guys were concerned. I'm sure it wasn't something Rex wanted spread around, and he knew he could trust me. I had a reputation for working hard, keeping my head down, and my nose out of any gossip. I didn't socialize much."

"Did anyone from HQ visit to inspect things or check on the cash accounting systems?"

Dale's forehead creased. "Not that I recall, but I'm not sure I would have known. I kept to my area. I know Rex had planned to visit with Frank when we were back in Nashville, especially after the accidents. He wanted to talk with him in person and share his concerns about the policy."

Coop asked a few more questions about Dax and like Buster, Dale had no idea the young man posing as Johnny was part of the Covington family. He hadn't seen anyone who didn't belong but confessed he was focused on the setup of the rides and had been working long hours. He did confirm how easy it would be to tamper with the pilot light and fill the RV with propane and how little time it would take to do it. "Once it's filled with the gas, all it needs is a spark and then kaboom."

Coop thanked him for his time and reminded him to get in touch if he thought of anything else that might be helpful.

While Coop studied his notes, AB came into his office, a cookie in her hand and another for him. She slumped into the chair, putting her legs over the side while she broke off a piece of cookie. "Bad news on Big Top. They don't have any records going back that far. The lady I talked to just chuckled and acted like I must have just fallen off the turnip truck to even ask such a thing. She politely told me they don't keep records going back that far, and nobody currently in the company had worked for them twenty-five years ago who could be of any help. She suggested I use the internet and dismissed me."

"Did she know you were working for a private investigator?"

AB threw her head back and laughed. "Of course not. She thinks I'm a journalist digging into the life of carnies and history of carnivals."

He grinned. "Silly of me to ask. You're such a convincing liar, it's scary sometimes. Good work." Over cookies, he briefed her on what he had learned from the two interviews. "We need to talk to Huck. He would have the most knowledge about the business aspects Dale mentioned. I also want to follow up with Frank. He never mentioned Rex talking to him about the accidents or the directive from corporate."

AB dusted the cookie crumbs from her fingers. "I called again and left another message. Maybe he's out of town?"

"Dig into him and see if we can find any relatives or anything else that could help us pin him down."

She extracted herself from the chair. "I'll tackle that first thing in the morning. I also got through to Alice, and she's willing to chat with you tonight. I sent her a link for a video call. Six o'clock our time works best for her. See you tomorrow." She reached out to rub Gus' nose before she left.

"Thanks, AB. Have a good night." Coop put the estate file

and his notebook in his leather briefcase, locked up the office, and loaded Gus into the Jeep.

Coop had time for a quick bite to eat before his call with Alice. He left Gus to help Aunt Camille and his dad clean up the dishes. As was his normal evening tradition, Gus stood by the dishwasher and made sure he wiped any lingering bits of food from each plate. Aunt Camille was usually a soft touch when it came to giving him a few extra bites of whatever meat they had for supper. With his focus on the stack of plates, Gus didn't even notice Coop leaving the room.

Coop settled in behind his desk and connected the call, waiting for Alice to join the conversation while reviewing the file AB had prepared. Alice lived outside of Dallas and was an accountant. After a few minutes, she popped onto the screen. "Hey, Alice, I appreciate you squeezing me in tonight."

She smiled and said, "No problem. I'm happy to help."

Coop went through the basics of his investigation and explained he was looking into the accidents and the fire at the carnival site that killed Frank's son. Alice nodded as he spoke.

"I remember that morning when I came to work. The day after the fire. It was just horrible. Everyone was so upset and worried."

Coop asked many of the same questions he had put forth to Bethany and Penny, and Alice confirmed their recollections. She had assisted in payroll and didn't add much knowledge of the maintenance records but also recalled Gavin wasn't in the office the morning after the fire.

Coop nodded and said, "Bethany thought you might be able to tell me more about Gavin."

Her smile faded. "He made it uncomfortable to work there." She sighed and continued, "It was my first real job, and I wanted to do everything right to make a good impression. He would come into my cubicle, and I wouldn't even know he was there until I got a weird feeling on the back of my neck. He was creepy and always remarked on what I was wearing or how he liked my hair. I just ignored him because I didn't want to cause a problem."

He frowned as he made a note. "Did it go beyond him talking to you and bothering you?"

She shrugged. "Not really. Sometimes he would put his head right on my shoulder as I worked and laugh, like it was fun. He asked me out constantly, and I always said no or that my parents didn't allow me to date older men. In reality, I guess he was only about four years older, but it was creepy."

"Did you tell Mr. Covington?"

She shook her head. "No, I didn't want to cause any problems and needed the job. I was embarrassed to even talk about it. Gavin's mom worked there, and she was Frank's assistant. I didn't want to make waves."

Coop thought back to the way things worked in that era. It had been commonplace for women, especially young ones new to the workforce, to put up with unwanted advances.

She added, "One day, I told Bethany about it, but it was right before the company was sold. There wasn't much that could be done. I wouldn't continue working with Gavin and had to find a new job anyway. She agreed it wouldn't matter at that point, and there was already so much chaos, it didn't make sense to whine to Frank about something trivial when he'd just lost his son."

"Obviously, Gavin left a negative impression on you. Outside of those inappropriate interactions, did you have an opinion about his work or his methods? Did you do any work directly for him?"

"I didn't do anything directly for him, but I didn't hold a high opinion of his work either. He was lazy, and he was impressed with himself, always remarking about his degree and how smart he was. He wasn't likeable. Everyone thought he just had the job because of his mom. I don't even think Huck liked him."

He asked her a few more questions about the corporate office, but her knowledge was limited to the payroll operations and nothing about the overall budget. She told him Huck was the person who could answer all those questions. "He knew the chart of accounts, income, and expenses off the top of his head. He was good at his job. As I went through school to become an accountant, I thought of Huck often. He was a natural."

Coop thanked her and asked her to get in touch if she remembered anything else before he disconnected their call.

He stared at his notes and circled Gavin's name. Not that being a sleazeball and a despicable human being were crimes, but Alice's statement added to the ugly painting that emerged when it came to Gavin's character.

14

Thursday was full of frustrations as AB was able to locate Huck's two daughters, who lived in the area but was greeted with only voicemail messages when she called the numbers she uncovered.

Coop spent most of the day absorbing the information he had learned from his interviews and research. Talking with Penny and Bethany had prompted more questions for Gavin and his absence from work the morning after the fire. If he were out visiting carnival sites, it would help to know where. Alice's recollections went more to Gavin's character in general than to any specific action related to the fire. AB shivered when he recounted Alice's statement. "I knew he was a pig that first day we met him. Men like him prey on the innocent, like Alice."

Penny's revelation about seeing Adele with Red was another issue that needed further investigation. That would be a sensitive one at best. He and AB brainstormed ideas and decided it was best to talk to Frank when he came in tomorrow to sign the estate paperwork. Coop wanted him informed before he probed deeper with Adele.

Talking with Buster and Dale gave even more credence to

Dax's theory about the accidents. Even though there was still no physical evidence to link the accidents and the fire, it was hard to write it off as a coincidence. Dax deserved to know they had corroborated his findings.

Late in the afternoon, AB came through Coop's office door with a smile. "Good news. Judge Monroe can see you tomorrow, first thing. You'll have to cut breakfast short or go earlier. She handed him the file she had prepared for the hearing.

"Thanks, AB. That's great. I'll make sure to drop your breakfast off before I head to court." He winked as he and Gus headed out the back door.

Friday morning, Coop was stirring sugar into his mug of coffee when Ben came through the door of Peg's Pancakes just after six o'clock. He whistled when he noticed Coop in a suit and tie. "Ah, you didn't think Judge Monroe would appreciate your DOES RUNNING LATE COUNT AS EXERCISE t-shirt?"

Coop dismissed his old friend's humor with a bat of his hand. After filling Ben's cup, Myrtle poised her pen on her order pad. "Blueberry waffles and pancakes are on special today. They come with eggs and bacon, if y'all are interested."

They both took her up on the suggestion. Ben rested against the back of the booth. Ben slid a folder across the table. "So, the exhumation is done. I faxed the documentation to your office last night but wasn't sure if you'd get it and thought you'd need it for court today." He reached for the sugar to add to his cup. "We kept it lowkey, and nobody seemed to pay much attention to what we were doing. Not saying somebody won't pick up on it, but at least we got it done without the press breathing down our necks."

Coop nodded and tapped the file folder. "Thanks for the report. It should be a quick hearing." He took a long sip of the rich brew he craved and sighed. "Frank's coming in today, so I'll be sure to let him know it's done."

"The cemetery crew removed the headstone and put it in storage. We thought there would be less interest if it were removed." He went on to say that a specialized forensic team would examine the remains, including a dental analysis and isotope profiles to try to narrow down the geographic area Nate could have come from. He hoped they might be able to match something on the dental comparisons to missing persons.

"I know Dax is disturbed that Nate, if that was even his actual name, was killed and that his family has been in the dark this whole time. AB and I worked yesterday trying to find a thread of anything in all our interviews and research that might lead to an answer to who might have been behind the fire. Without any physical evidence, it's tough to get to the bottom of it all."

"Welcome to the world of cold cases. Speaking of... any progress on my box?"

Coop shook his head. "Haven't even started. AB and I are focused on this Covington thing. Madison and Ross are doing some side jobs and taking some time off until business picks up a bit."

Myrtle arrived with their breakfast, and Coop added hot syrup to his waffles. "All the digging we've done so far reinforces Dax's theory that the information he learned about the accidents and shady maintenance had a direct correlation to the fire in his RV. I'm certain somebody in Frank's office intercepted that message and took action to protect whatever was going on with the false records. I'm convinced Dax was right and had every reason to disappear."

"Poor guy gave up his life and all those years with his family. Whoever is behind all this is beyond heartless."

"We need to find Huck Grover. He was in charge of the business side of Frank's company for years, and he's bound to know something. Or he's involved in it up to his ears. AB found his adult daughters, but no answer at their homes either."

Ben's phone rang and after a few clipped words, he shoveled the last of his breakfast into his mouth. "Gotta run."

Coop held up his hand as soon as Ben dug into his back pocket for his wallet. "My turn. We haven't done anything on your cases, so you've got a reprieve on breakfast this week."

Ben grinned and slipped into his coat as he hurried for the door.

Coop settled back and finished his breakfast at a leisurely pace while he waited for AB's order and savored a third cup of coffee. Technically, it was more like two cups at the most. Peg's cups were smaller than his normal oversized mug, and Myrtle always refilled it before it was empty.

He paid the check and carried the takeout order to the Jeep where Gus was waiting. Despite it being earlier than normal, they found AB at her desk and placed her takeout breakfast in front of her.

She finished typing an email and turned to Coop. "Good news, I was just firming up a contract for some background work for a manufacturing firm Chandler Hollund referred to us. They want us to do a security assessment and handle all the backgrounds for their employees."

Coop clapped his hands together. "That's great news. Is it enough work to keep Madison and Ross busy?"

"It's a large firm with over two hundred employees, so yes, and it's a great contract in that they tend to have some turnover, so we'll have ongoing business." She opened the box and sniffed the pancakes.

"Music to my ears. Let Madison and Ross know they can start back next week, and we should be able to at least keep them busy for half days, especially if they've got some other work lined up already. Tell them just to come when it works for them."

Coop made sure AB had a copy of Ben's report while Gus shimmied as close as he could to AB, who was always good for at least a bite or two of her breakfast. "This should be quick, so I should be back within an hour," Coop said, as he left through the back door and drove downtown to the courthouse. After parking in the garage, he made his way to Judge Monroe's courtroom and stopped by to thank his clerk for getting him on the calendar so quickly.

As Coop suspected, the hearing took only a few minutes, and he left with the paperwork that restored Dax to a legally living person. He didn't want there to be any issues with the new estate paperwork, and the judge's ruling would shore up any chance of someone deciding to try to fight Dax's status, since technically a death certificate had declared him dead twenty-five years ago.

He rewarded himself with a quick stop at a coffee shop for a latte and then drove back to the office. Coop settled into his desk and made a few notes for the upcoming meeting with Frank.

When he finished, he turned to his computer and scanned his email. His eyes narrowed as he read one message. "You've got to be kidding me."

He rested his head against the back of his chair and sighed. About that time, AB came through the door. "What's wrong?"

"Marlene."

"What now?" she asked, sinking into a chair.

"The lawyer just emailed and said she went to visit Marlene to let her know about the motel where she could stay when she gets out on Monday, so she could do her community service. Seems Marlene, in her infinite wisdom, rejected the offer outright and has plans to stay at Ruben's place. He's the guy who got arrested with her."

AB shook her head. "That woman. I have no words."

"Ms. Flint is always polite, but I can tell she's at the end of her rope. She tried to explain to Marlene that associating with Ruben wasn't in her best interest. He's been in trouble before and is known to the local authorities as a nuisance criminal." Coop took a sip from his latte. "Nuisance and criminal are two of the kinder words I can think of to describe my mother."

"She'll end up back in jail if she doesn't follow through on her community service. I suspect that judge has lost any semblance of restraint by now."

Coop shook his head. "I don't have time for her nonsense and like Ms. Flint said, Marlene hasn't picked up on the fact Ruben got out of jail before her and didn't bother to visit or attempt to bail her out."

AB rolled her eyes. "You've done all you can do, Coop. How many times have you been through something like this with her? She's not going to change."

"I know. I just hate waiting for the next drama to erupt. I honestly don't know how Dad put up with her at all."

"Charlie is a saint, and I imagine he put his children first and did his best to insulate you and your brother from her bad behavior. You're not responsible for her. She's the only one who holds the power to change her attitude and her actions."

Coop stared at his cup. "I know that up here." He tapped his forehead. "But it hurts here." He moved his hand to his chest. "You'd think by now, I'd be used to her bull...oney." He smirked and shrugged.

AB laughed. "I've heard the word before. She makes me want to knock some sense into her. Literally. So, I understand the language, believe me."

Coop positioned his hands over his keyboard. "Well, it's not Ms. Flint's fault. She's done all she can do. Come Monday, Marlene will be loose in Vermont, and who knows what trouble she'll find next."

AB left him to stew and finish his email. A few minutes later, Coop heard her greeting Frank, Dax, and Lindsay. Frank was still apologizing as they came down the hallway. "I hope it's okay, but I wanted Dax and Lindsay here so they could ask questions."

AB smiled at him. "Not a problem at all. Come on in and have a seat at the conference table. I'll bring some tea and coffee for you in a few minutes." Coop had changed the whiteboard to a stunning photo of the Smoky Mountains in preparation for the meeting and stood to greet the three of them.

They gathered around the table with warm beverages and cookies as Coop updated them on the exhumation and his success in court just a few hours ago. He let Dax enjoy the news of his return to life, and they all joked a bit about it before Coop broached the more serious topic.

"Interestingly, I also talked with a couple of the workers who were onsite at the time of the RV fire, and one of them, who was in charge of maintenance, confirmed what Dax suspected. Rex told him he had received messages from corporate suggesting they cut back on maintenance and replacement parts, and his bonus would be tied to that metric. Turns out Rex didn't want any part of it and made sure to keep up the maintenance as normal, even going so far as to skim a little off the concessions to use for purchasing parts."

Frank brought his fingers to his temples. "That makes me sick. It wasn't from me; I can assure you. God bless Rex for not listening to that nonsense. That division was our biggest, and that could have proven to be even worse than the other accidents. Rex had a good head on his shoulders and was the best, which is why he ran my largest division."

Coop nodded. "One of the workers said Rex planned to see you in person when his division circled back to Nashville. That, of course, would have been after the fire. Did Rex ever come to talk to you?"

Frank shook his head. "No, I wasn't functioning very well after the fire, but I would have remembered meeting with Rex.

Everyone was staying away from me or insulating me. I'm not sure which, but it makes sense that Rex would have avoided a business conversation. He came to Dax's funeral, but we never talked about the accidents." Frank brought his hand to his forehead. "I had hoped what Dax found wasn't true, but at the same time, deep inside, I knew there had to be something to it. Huck and Marvin were the only two people who carried enough weight to communicate with the bosses like that." His voice cracked, and tears filled his eyes. "I wish one of them would have come to me about it. Maybe I could have stopped all of this awfulness from happening."

Dax sighed, placed his hand on top of his father's arm, and met Coop's eyes. "I'm relieved to hear you corroborated what I had discovered. I thought I had made it up or remembered it wrong. Had I not called Dad and left that message, I never would have thought he was behind it, but at that point, it was fight or flight, and I was all about the flying."

"You're not to blame, son. Not at all. I just hope I live long enough to allow Mr. Harrington to get to the bottom of it all."

Coop took a sip of coffee before he turned his attention to the estate documents, outlining and confirming Frank's wishes. "Adele will get a lump sum payout, as will Gavin. The family home and acreage will go to Dax, and Lindsay will keep her house that Frank bought for her. Adele will also receive a smaller home that's currently a rental property. The tenants will be given a ninety-day notice as will Adele, so she can vacate the family home and move into the rental house. She will also retain all her jewelry, personal belongings, some specific household items, and her Mercedes."

Coop glanced up at Frank. "Is Adele aware of this new provision?"

Frank shook his head. "Not yet. I plan to tell her soon."

Coop glanced back down at the paperwork. "Currently, Frank and Lindsay are listed as the corporate officers of the insurance company. We've added Dax as an officer today and will file the new paperwork. Upon Frank's death, the insurance company will transfer to Lindsay and Dax. Gavin will keep his current job and salary until such time as he decides to leave." Coop looked across the table at Lindsay and Dax. "Should you decide to terminate him, he'll be given a generous severance package as outlined in the document." They both nodded their heads.

Frank interrupted Coop. "I've explained to Dax that I didn't want to burden Lindsay with the business. I know it would be too much for her, so I had intended for Gavin to be in charge of it. With Dax home, he can run it, and he and Lindsay can work together or sell it or whatever they want to do. Gavin knows the business inside and out, so he'll be an asset, but he can be a handful. I don't want to set anything up where you two are stuck with him. I also want to be fair to Gavin and reward him for all his years of loyalty."

Dax reached across and patted his dad's arm. "I understand, Dad. Whatever you want and think is best works for me."

Coop highlighted the next section. "The remaining vehicles, including the Mustang, will go to Dax, along with a specific account Frank set up for Dax to allow him to pursue his college education." Frank smiled while tears shined in Dax's eyes. Coop continued, "Frank's investment accounts, stocks, bonds, properties, and all other assets will be split between Dax and Lindsay, equally."

Frank tapped his finger on the table. "We'll stop by the bank on the way home and get Dax to sign onto the accounts. Right now, Lindsay and I are the signatories."

Coop made sure there were no questions before he had Frank sign multiple copies of the documents, and AB notarized them.

After he signed everything, Frank sat back in his chair and sighed. "I feel so much better knowing all that is taken care of.

I'm not sure what I would have done if I had died and left this all in a mess."

"No need to worry. We'll get the corporate changes filed today. You can keep your signed copies, and we'll retain a copy here in our office."

Frank smiled at his two children and nodded. "Lindsay's birthday is next week and with Dax home, I've decided it's high time we have a little party at the house. I hope you and Annabelle will come and celebrate with us. If not for you, I wouldn't have my boy back with me, and Lindsay deserves a bit of fun on her special day. We'd be honored if you would consider attending."

Coop glanced at AB, who dipped her head in agreement. "We'd love to come. You can give AB the details, and she'll make sure to remind me."

"Splendid. Shall we go and celebrate with lunch?" He reached for Lindsay's hand.

Coop held up a finger. "I just need a word with Frank. It will only take a minute."

Dax stood. "Of course. We'll give AB all the details about the party and meet you out front, Dad."

After they left, Coop met Frank's eyes. "This is indelicate, at best, but during my interviews, I found a witness who saw Adele having drinks with Red Fulton in December, just months before the accidents in the spring the following year. From what I gathered, Red came to town a few times a year and stopped by to persuade you to sell Royal. This was after he had been to your offices."

Frank's shoulders sagged. "I don't know anything about Adele having drinks with him. Red did come by every few months and always made a point of trying to convince me to retire and sell him the business. It had almost become a joke, since he knew I wasn't interested in selling. I can only guess he thought if he wined and dined Adele, she might be able to influence me to sell. I can tell you… it wouldn't have worked. Adele was never shy about making it clear she was looking for male companionship. I don't have a recollection of anything she said about Red, and she never made a case for him buying the place."

Coop ran his finger over his notepad. "I just wanted you to understand that I'll be following up with Adele. I didn't want you to be caught off-guard if it upsets her."

Frank chuckled. "I think those papers I just signed have a far better chance of upsetting her. Don't say anything about it when you see her. I need to find the right time to tell her, and Lindsay and Dax want to be there with me. It's complicated with a second wife, but I think she'll understand with Dax home how important it is to me."

"I won't say a word about it. I'm bound by attorney-client privilege and wouldn't discuss it anyway. That's a private, family matter. Trust me, I know how complicated families can be."

Frank stood and extended his hand to Coop. "I can't thank you enough…for everything."

Coop followed him down the hallway, where they found Dax and Lindsay waiting in the reception area. "All set?" asked Dax.

Frank nodded and turned to AB. "We look forward to seeing you at the party."

Coop and AB watched as Lindsay and Dax each linked arms with their dad and led him outside to the car. AB stared out the window, watching them. "It's such a shame to think this is probably the happiest Frank has been in the last twenty-five years, and he knows it's all going to end soon."

15

After a relaxing weekend of cards and a movie binge with Aunt Camille and his dad, Coop took a ride over to Covington Insurance Services on Monday morning. Coop opened the glass door of the well-appointed office and took a few steps across the plush carpet to the large wooden reception desk. The polite secretary greeted him with a friendly smile, and Coop asked to see Gavin.

She used the intercom and moments later, Gavin strolled from around the corner. "Mr. Harrington, the illustrious private detective who returned the beloved Dax from the dead. What can I do for you? More questions?"

Coop ignored his sarcasm. "That's exactly why I'm here. Do you have a few minutes?"

Gavin motioned him to a conference room, where Coop took a chair and opened his notebook.

Gavin sat across from Coop and raised his brows. "I don't have much time, so I hope this can be quick."

"I talked to several witnesses last week and learned that you were out of town visiting carnival sites at the time of the RV fire in Georgia. I was hoping that might refresh your memory, and you could tell me where you were?"

Gavin laughed. "I have no idea. I could have been visiting sites, and I could have been at the office. I don't remember. Like I said before, twenty-five years is a long time ago, and nothing sticks in my mind either way."

"Really?" Coop asked. "Your mother was planning to marry Frank, and he gets word his son has died, and you don't remember anything about it? You don't remember your mom calling you to tell you or what you did at work? It seems like that would be a memorable event."

Gavin threw his head back and gazed at the ceiling, his hands clasped across his chest. He jerked his head back to face Coop. "I got nothing. You've got to remember; I was young and not that dialed into all the happenings in the office. Those people were not exactly in my social circle."

Coop resisted the urge to reach out and wipe the smirk off Gavin's face. "Is it true Huck sent you out to the sites to audit their cash procedures?"

He rolled his eyes. "Oh, yes. He had me traipsing around to all these backwater towns so I could do surprise inspections." He chuckled. "That was sort of fun. They were always annoyed and sometimes nervous to have me watching over their procedures and double counting their cash receipts to make sure they matched. Huck didn't want me to tell them who I was until the ticket booth closed, so I'd just hang around dressed in jeans and a t-shirt and watch them and the concessions to see if I spotted anything unusual and then introduce myself at the end of the night."

"Did you happen to visit Rex Fulton's division in Georgia? He ran the biggest division, correct? I would think that would warrant an inspection."

Gavin frowned. "They all sort of run together. I'm sure I

could have visited that division since I primarily went to sites in Tennessee, Georgia, Kentucky, and would sometimes dip into North Carolina or Alabama. Huck wanted me to stay within driving distance to keep our expenses low."

"I would think you would remember going to the site where Frank's son died in a fire." Coop stared at Gavin.

"But he didn't really die in that fire, did he? For all we know, he could have set the fire himself. He's been hiding out for the last twenty-five years and shows up now for what? To collect on his inheritance?" The bitterness in Gavin's voice came through with each word.

"Getting back to you that day, you don't remember being on the road when you got the news or having been at that particular carnival site where the fire took place?"

Gavin shook his head. "I don't remember. I think I would, had I been there at the time of the fire. I very well could have been on the road, and the person you talked to must have a very good memory to recall I wasn't in the office. I could have been anywhere."

Coop sat back in his chair. "Were you happy when your mom and Frank married? Did it come as a surprise?"

Gavin grinned. "If Mom's happy, I'm happy. I learned that a long time ago. It wasn't a real surprise. They'd been spending lots of time together, and she was very attentive to Lindsay. It seemed like a natural progression." He blew out a breath. "Frank's been good to me. I can't complain. Now, with Dax back from the dead…who knows?"

"You mentioned Huck was concerned with keeping expenses low. Was that a general theme with him, always looking to cut costs?"

Gavin's brow creased deeper. "Well, that's a priority for a good business manager. I think that's part of the reason he liked to send me out to audit the receipts. It kept everyone on their toes and discouraged skimming. It was a cash business, which made it easy for employees to steal. With the tickets, we had some semblance of tracking, but with the concessions, all we had to go by was inventory, and there was room for error. Huck was old-fashioned, but he knew how to keep a business profitable and kept us focused on tracking and evaluating everything."

"Did you stay in touch with Huck after he left the company?"

Gavin grimaced, like he'd stepped in something disgusting. "No, why would I? We had nothing in common, and I didn't need him for anything." Gavin quickly added, "Like a reference or anything. Frank just slid me into that job once he left."

"I've been interviewing everyone that worked in the office at the time. Do you remember a young woman who worked with Bethany named Alice?"

A lecherous grin appeared as Gavin nodded. "Oh, yes, how could I forget her. She was a beauty. I wonder what ever happened to her?"

"She's a very successful accountant. Has her MBA and a wonderful family. She mostly recalled your clumsy attempts to persuade her to date you and the creepy way you would appear behind her."

Gavin's eyes hardened, and he shook his head. "She must be thinking of someone else."

"No, I'm sure it was you." Coop closed the cover on his notebook. "Thanks for your time, again. If you happen to remember anything more about the days surrounding the fire, give me a call." He stood. "I'll show myself out."

Coop smiled at the secretary and wished her a good day on his way out the door. Age often mellowed a man, but Coop found Gavin to be unlikeable and couldn't imagine how much worse he probably was when he was younger. He gripped the steering wheel of the Jeep tighter as he recalled his condescending tone and his creepy grin when he mentioned Alice.

Soon enough, he pulled into the parking lot behind his office and once inside, he poured a cup of decaf AB had kindly brewed. He took a sip and sauntered to her desk, where Gus lounged next to her. She turned from the computer screen and raised her brows. "Well, did you learn anything?"

He sank into the couch and took a long swallow from his cup. "I'm glad you weren't there with me; you might have slugged him. He's a piece of work. Under all his arrogance, there's a strong vein of jealousy toward Dax. He even went so far as to suggest Dax set the fire. When he finds out Dax will be his new boss, he'll be unhinged."

"So, his memory wasn't jogged after you confronted him with the fact that he wasn't in the office?"

Coop shook his head. "Claims he doesn't remember but would remember if he had been at the site of the fire." Coop swallowed more coffee. "He's disgusting, and I don't trust him, but if he was involved in setting the fire, it's going to be hard to prove anything."

AB sighed. "With him being the only person missing from the office, it shines a bright light of suspicion on him. Not to mention, he's beyond unlikeable."

"Ah, if that was a crime, we'd have way too many people in jail." Coop chuckled as he cradled his cup. "So, are you saying Gavin intercepted the message and drove down to Georgia intent on silencing Dax?"

She shrugged. "I don't know. A young kid like that. Sounds like he was just as unlikeable then, but murder is a big step. Maybe someone directed him to do it? Would he come up with that on his own?"

Coop shrugged. "Most people pegged him as lazy, so it seems ambitious, but maybe he was directed."

AB's eyes narrowed. "But then wouldn't he have just given the person up now?"

Coop grinned. "Not if he thinks it's unsolvable. No point in confessing if you think you can get away with it. Honestly, I'm not sure we'll ever be able to prove it. There is no physical evidence that still exists."

"That's never deterred us before." AB stood and took her cup to the kitchen for a refill.

Coop followed her. "I think I'll have some lunch. I'll need the fortification before I tackle Adele. I can only imagine how she'll react to my questions about her night of cozy drinks with Red."

After some delicious leftovers from Aunt Camille's Sunday dinner, Coop left Gus with AB and set out for Frank's house. He pulled into the huge driveway, noticing the six-car garage of the massive brick home that graced the acreage. Living in Belle Meade, Coop was no stranger to the elaborate homes and mansions throughout the neighborhood, and Frank's home was no exception.

Thankful he had worn a nice shirt today instead of one of the t-shirts he preferred, he made his way up the brick stairs to the thick double wooden-door entrance and rang the bell. After several minutes, Adele opened the door. "Mr. Harrington, this is a surprise."

"I apologize for not calling ahead but was on my way back to the office and had a question for you. Do you have a few minutes?"

"Of course. Come on in." She held the door wide, and he took in the high ceilings of the impressive entry. She led him through it and to the huge living space, outfitted with two couches and several chairs positioned around the large fire-place. "I was just in the family room off the kitchen. We can chat in there. I was having a cup of tea and doing some paperwork, would you like one?"

"That would be great, thank you." She pointed him to a room off the open kitchen where a flat-screen television was tuned to a daytime drama. He took a seat in an overstuffed chair and waited for his hostess.

Minutes later, she returned with a tea tray. "Frank's spending a few hours at the office this afternoon. He thinks the world of you, and I must apologize again for my lack of manners when you came to the condo in Florida. I was just in shock, I think."

Coop accepted the cup she offered. "No need to apologize. This is a unique case, and I'm sure the news was startling."

She smiled and took a seat. "So, what can I do for you today?"

Coop set his cup on the coffee table. "I'm afraid I have to ask you a rather indelicate question." Her brows rose over the rim of her cup, and he continued. "As you know, we've been interviewing former employees and anyone connected to Royal twenty-five years ago. In those discussions, we discovered a witness who saw you at the Oak Bar at the Hermitage Hotel in December, a few months before the accidents. You were with Red Fulton, just the two of you. You can understand with his interest in buying Royal, it begs the question as to the nature of your relationship and that particular evening."

She smiled and then laughed, almost giggling. "Oh my, I'd forgotten about that outing with Red. Well, you see, it's all quite innocent. Red came through Nashville a few times a year, always coming to see Frank and doing his best to convince Frank to sell Royal to him. Frank wanted no part of it and rejected his offers. It had become a ritual and although they were rivals in business, the two seemed to get along well." She sighed. "Anyway, Red invited me to join him for a drink, to celebrate the holiday season. It was just an after work, grab a drink to toast the season thing. Nothing nefarious, trust me."

She had a friendly lilt to her voice, and her blue eyes shimmered. She was charming, and Coop could only imagine what she had been like in her youth. Irresistible came to mind. He nodded. "That's what I figured, but like I said, we're following up on everything. Was that something you had done before? Drinks with Red?"

She ran her finger over the rim of her cup. "I can't recall another time." She smiled and added, "Not that he hadn't asked." The purring cat the ladies had described came to mind.

"So, what made you accept his invitation that night?"

She shrugged. "Weakness and the holidays, I suppose. The Hermitage is hard to resist, and it's always decorated so beautifully for Christmas. It's not a place a single woman with a secretary's salary could afford. Like I said, it wasn't anything more than a friendly drink."

"Did you tell Frank about the meeting or think he would be upset if you were seeing Red outside the office?"

She shook her head. "No, it wasn't important, and I didn't mention it. Frank and I weren't a couple at the time. You understand this was before Laura Beth died?"

Coop nodded. "Oh yes, I didn't mean tell him because of your romantic relationship. I meant more as a courtesy to let him know you were spending time with the competition, just in case someone saw you, that sort of thing."

She shook her head, her smile fading a bit. "I didn't think of it like that. Like I said, Red and Frank were friendly toward each other."

"During the conversation, did Red ask you about the business or suggest you could help him acquire it? Maybe try to get some inside information from you?"

Hers eyes widened. "No, nothing like that. He made no secret of wanting to buy Royal and like I told you before, he had a keen interest in it but never pumped me for information. I still can't imagine him orchestrating those accidents. I mean, who would purposely harm people, children especially, over business?"

"It's just that Red was the beneficiary of all of those tragic events that befell Frank and Royal, so it's a natural conclusion."

Coop was mesmerized at the fact that her face remained immovable. He had to watch her lips and her eyes, since every other part of her face was expressionless. "I can see how he would be a prime suspect for the accidents, but I would have a hard time imagining he would do such a thing. I know it looks bad and that he ended up with Royal, but I honestly don't think he was involved, and he never asked me for inside information. I think he hoped I could help charm Frank into considering, but that was it."

"After the accidents, how long did it take for Red to visit and make another offer?"

She leaned back against the cushion. "Oh my. Let's see, the accidents happened in the spring, and everything was such a blur with all the investigations and lawyers; it was just awful. I don't remember him showing up again until summer, maybe." She sat up straighter. "Yes, it was after Laura Beth died. He visited and offered Frank his condolences. That was a very quick and low-key visit. I honestly don't even remember if he brought up buying the company at that point. With the loss of Laura Beth and all the stress from the lawsuits, Frank was in a daze. Not to mention, it would have been very poor form."

Coop turned back several pages in his notebook. "You and Frank married in November, not too long after he lost his wife and just a couple months after the fire in Dax's RV. They always say not to make decisions when under stress. Did that worry you that you were moving too quickly?"

She smiled. "I know it seems fast, but I had known Frank a very long time, and we were a great match. Plus, it just broke my heart that Lindsay was so distraught. She needed someone to watch over her. She was quite close to her mother and Dax, so her whole world had been turned upside down." She took a sip of tea. "If I'm being honest, I'd always admired Frank, and he relied on me. We had a very close relationship, so it was an easy shift to become partners in marriage." She looked around the magnificent space surrounding her. "We've had a wonderful marriage, and I've been blessed."

Tears filled her eyes. "I'm trying not to even think about what I know is coming and how I'll go on without Frank. I know it's inevitable, but I keep hoping for a miracle. I can't imagine being on my own in this big, old house." She dabbed at the corners of her eyes with the edge of her napkin.

Coop took note of the fact that Frank hadn't informed her of the updated estate documents. "Frank is a wonderful man. I'm glad he was able to reunite with his son and only wish it could have happened sooner. I know it pains them both to think of all that time lost."

"Well, that's Dax's fault. He was foolish enough to believe his father was behind the fire." Her now-clipped voice had lost its lilt.

"So, from what you've told me, it's safe to say you deny working with Red to help him sabotage Royal and ultimately buy the company, correct?"

She brought her hand to her throat. "Yes, Mr. Harrington. It's very safe to say that I didn't help Red and by the time the sale took place, Frank had lost all interest in Royal and was ready to walk away from it. Red offered him a fair price. While I realize in your line of work you have to ask such ridiculous questions, to say I'm insulted would be an understatement."

Coop nodded and closed his notebook. "I understand and as I said, I knew the topic wouldn't be welcome, but we're determined to follow all leads, no matter where they take us."

Her lips thinned as she pressed them together when Coop stood. "Thank you for the tea, Mrs. Covington. I look forward to seeing you at Lindsay's party this weekend. Frank extended the invitation."

She glanced at the stack of papers on the coffee table. "Yes, he told me you and your assistant will be coming. I'm just finalizing the arrangements today."

She started to rise from the couch, but he held up his hand. "I can see myself out. Enjoy the rest of your day."

16

Tuesday morning after catching up with Ross and Madison who were back in the office for a few hours each day, Coop and AB gathered around the conference table and stared at the glass board, reviewing all the notes and clues they had gathered. AB pointed at Gavin's name. "Like I said yesterday, he's the only one who could have been at the carnival site. We've accounted for everyone else being at the office."

Coop nodded and kept staring. "Right, unless whoever set the fire was hired by someone at the office. That opens up the suspect list to anyone who worked there and had access to the answering machine in Frank's office."

"So, we're back to square one." AB sighed. "I left another message for Huck and one on each of his daughters' phones, hoping someone will call us back."

Coop homed in on Adele's name on the board. He had added a note about the undercurrent he felt when he talked to her. "She and her son share a resentment toward Dax that doesn't make much sense."

"Don't you think they're just worried about their stake in the inheritance? They could easily control Lindsay, I think, but Dax is stronger and clearly the apple of his dad's eye. They probably see the writing on the wall."

Coop continued to stare at the board. "And unless Adele was acting yesterday, she doesn't have a clue about the new terms of Frank's will. Even though the prenuptial stipulates she isn't entitled to any of the family property, he must have made some promises to her over the years, or she has assumed she'll stay in the house."

AB's brows arched. "He's probably waiting until after the party to avoid any problems. I think he wants the event to be special for Lindsay and Dax."

The phone ringing cut their theory session short. AB answered it from Coop's desk. Coop's head jerked around when she said, "Yes, I'll accept the charges."

Only one person always called the office collect—Marlene.

He listened and shook his head, making exaggerated hand gestures so AB would understand. "Sorry, Marlene," she said, "Coop's out of the office. Would you like me to have him call you?"

The squawk of his mother's voice was so loud, he could make out most of what she was saying. After she ranted on about not being able to find Ruben and having to break into his house so she could have a place to stay, she ended with making sure AB understood it was an emergency. She must speak to Coop the minute he returned.

AB jotted a phone number on a sticky note and promised she would let Coop know. She replaced the receiver and handed him the note.

He took it as his head throbbed. "I told you the minute she got out of jail, she would be a problem. Now, here we are twenty-four hours later. Did I hear her say she broke into Ruben's house?"

AB gritted her teeth. "Yes, seems he's not home like she

expected, and she waited around and broke in yesterday, so she'd have a place to stay."

"She's lucky she isn't back in jail." Coop stabbed his finger on the bright orange note. "I'll call that motel up there that Ms. Flint suggested and see if they have a room available before I call her back. I don't have time for Marlene's drama right now."

He picked up his coffee and sloshed it on his t-shirt. He grimaced and dabbed at it with a napkin, thankful he was wearing a dark-brown shirt. He couldn't help but laugh when he noticed the words on it—PATIENCE IS A VIRTUE JUST NOT ONE OF MINE.

AB left the room, and Gus burrowed into his chair while Coop rifled through the notes on his desk, looking for the name of the motel. He found it on a legal pad and after a quick conversation, he learned they had vacancies and could accommodate his mother for the next three weeks.

He took a deep breath and sat back in his chair, gazing out the window. Moments later, AB returned with a steaming cup of coffee. Real coffee from the aroma. With a wink, she set it and a cookie in front of him. "I figure you could use this right about now. I'm making an exception to the one cup rule, but just for today."

He reached for the oversized mug he always used. "Bless you, AB. I honestly don't know what I would do without you." He took several swallows and shut his eyes, letting the strong brew work its magic. After a couple bites of the cookie and more coffee, he reached for the phone and dialed the Vermont number.

"Mom, AB said you called."

"I'm in a right mess here. Ruben is nowhere to be found, and I was set to stay with him while I complete this stupid community service. You know… that judge had it in for me from the start."

"What is it you need?" Coop asked, concentrating on keeping the irritation from his voice.

"I need you to fix this for me," she screeched.

He slowly counted to ten, but only got to five. "There's no fixing it. You have to stay and do your community service. You cannot break into someone's home, or you will end up in jail again."

"I have a good mind to just leave this backwater town. It's been nothing but trouble for me."

"If you don't stay and complete the terms of your sentence, they'll issue a warrant for your arrest. You just need to put in the hours and be done."

"I am far too old to be picking up trash or cleaning up after people. Ms. Flint, that idiot lawyer you hired, gave me the list of places I could work, and they're all horrid. That's no place for a woman of my age."

Coop almost chewed a hole through his tongue. "Ms. Flint was trying to help you by getting things in place for you to complete your hours. The duties available for people completing their community service are not highly sought-after positions. It's typically crummy work that nobody likes to do. You just need to swallow your pride and get it done."

"Don't you tell me to swallow my pride. I'm still your mother and deserve some respect. What good is it having a son who's a lawyer if you can't get me out of this little problem. You must be a sorry excuse for one."

His heart hammered in his throat. "You've been through the judicial process, and you've been sentenced. The time for lawyers is over. It's now the time for you to pay for what you did. If you'd rather be in jail, I'm sure that could be arranged."

"Don't sass me, young man."

Coop remained silent and counted to ten again. He didn't get to three before Marlene's voice shrieked in his ear. "I'm not sure how I can be expected to volunteer my time to work for free, while I have no money for food and no place to stay. Answer me that one, smart guy."

"As Ms. Flint told you, I was willing to pay for your motel room for a couple of weeks so you could get your community service done. The motel includes breakfast, and one of those jobs on the list was washing dishes at the senior center. You'd get a meal while you worked and one to take home with you. That solves both problems, but you rejected that idea, intent on staying with the criminal friend of yours, who it seems isn't home."

"I'm sure something important came up. Ruben wouldn't just leave me in a lurch like that."

"Your choices are limited. Either you figure out a way to do your community service, or you go to jail."

"You're no help at all," she hollered.

"What's it going to be? I have work to do and need to get going."

"Fine. Call the damned lawyer and tell her to set it all up at the senior center. I can't believe you're too cold hearted to do anything to help me."

"So, paying for your motel room, that's not helping you? You're unbelievable. Just get yourself to Ms. Flint's office, and I'll call her." He slammed the phone down before she could say anything else.

Coop flicked the top of the pen he was holding and stared at the phone. He turned to AB and shook his head. "We need to change my office number so she can't call me anymore."

AB grinned. "I'll get on it. And by that, I mean I'll call Ms. Flint and get her prepared to handle the motel and try to get Marlene on board with the senior center. I'll make sure she only authorizes payment one day at a time in case Marlene flakes."

Coop eased back into his chair. "You read my mind, AB. Thanks."

After staring at the board for more than thirty minutes and

getting nowhere, Coop tidied up the conference table and his desk, whistled for Gus to follow, and flicked off the lights in his office.

AB was hanging up the phone when they passed by her desk. "Aunt Camille has book club, so Dad and I have plans to have a poker game with a couple of his friends from the community center, and Ben is joining us. I'm going to duck out early. I can't concentrate anyway. I think I'll take Gus to the park so I can calm down before I go home. I don't want to burden Dad or Aunt Camille with the latest from Mom."

At the sound of one his favorite words, Gus' ears perked, and he stood at attention in front of Coop, his tail wagging back and forth across the hardwood floor.

Coop smiled down at him. "You're always up for a nice walk in the park, aren't you, buddy?"

AB smiled at Coop and patted the top of Gus' head. "Sounds good. Ms. Flint is going to handle things in Vermont. Try to enjoy your evening, Coop."

17

Wednesday was better in that Coop didn't hear from Marlene. After a day like yesterday, he was glad he refused to give her his cell phone number. There would be no escape if she had easy access to him. He tried to push away the guilt that always followed an altercation with his mother. She made it difficult to feel anything but despise and resentment toward her.

Gus had a checkup at the vet office, so Coop spent part of his morning there and when they returned to the office, Gus was worn out from all the social interaction and sniffing every surface of the place. Coop had worn his new DON'T STOP RETRIEVIN' t-shirt with the golden retriever on it since he knew everyone at the vet's office would like it.

Gus passed out for a nap and over leftovers from last night's pokerfest, Coop and AB batted around a few ideas about the case. Coop mentioned again the fact that someone other than Gavin could have been involved and intercepted the call and then paid someone to get rid of Dax.

"That brings us back to Marvin, Penny, Bethany, and Huck, who we haven't interviewed yet, not to mention the other clerks that worked there. Speaking of Huck, I need to do a bit more research into him. His current home is in a high-end neighborhood and worth a few bucks, but he also retired at a high level, which means he was making an excellent salary. Leaving Royal was a good move for him."

Coop tapped his pen on his notepad. "Don't forget Adele. She did her best to explain away meeting Red at the Oak Bar, but the fact that she agreed to join him and the timing, just months before the accidents, is odd."

AB bobbed her head. "None of the people we've looked into live an extravagant lifestyle. The only two who do are Gavin and Adele. I wonder if she received any kind of influx of cash during that time. The only motive I see is monetary, as in Red paying her to help him gain control of the company. Even if we could find her bank from twenty-five years ago, they wouldn't have records going that far back."

"Let's dig into her a bit deeper. Look at any property in her name prior to marrying Frank and do the same with Gavin. Let's see if either of them acquired property around that time or if their financial situation changed. Let's also see if we can find any of her friends outside of coworkers who might know more about her, maybe someone from when she was married to Gavin's dad."

AB nodded. "I'll start searching."

Coop reviewed the backgrounds AB had prepared on all the people they knew of who worked in the Royal offices at the time of the fire, and nothing popped out at him. Gavin had gone to college in Knoxville and was the recipient of several scholarships and grants based on need. Adele's earnings as a single mom made him eligible for assistance, and living in a modest house had allowed her to pay for what the scholarships didn't cover. After Adele's husband died, she had continued to live in Murfreesboro, just over thirty miles from Nashville, and she had stayed there until she married Frank.

From looking at the property records, Adele sold the family home and then bought Gavin his first house, which he later sold and had since moved several times, always buying something bigger and more expensive. All of that seemed normal. Lots of parents helped their kids buy their first home.

There was little difference between the amount Adele sold her home for and the amount she paid for Gavin's new house, which was in both their names. Nothing indicated an influx of funds from an outside source.

In the late afternoon, AB came through Coop's door with a sticky note. "I found Adele's neighbor in Murfreesboro. A Mrs. Davis still lives in the same house next to Adele's place. I called her, and she's happy to meet with you first thing tomorrow morning.

Thursday morning, Coop made the trip to Murfreesboro and found Adele's old neighborhood, where Mrs. Davis still lived. She welcomed Coop into her small ranch style home, on a street filled with similar houses.

The years hadn't been as gentle to her as they had been to Adele. Mrs. Davis toddled, as if her knees hurt, and her short gray hair didn't have much style. She smiled at Coop, which accentuated the deep wrinkles in her face. Not a speck of makeup adorned her face, and her blue eyes twinkled as she offered Coop a cup of coffee.

He accepted the flowered mug with gratitude and joined her at the dining table off her small kitchen. "I appreciate you seeing me on such short notice, Mrs. Davis. I'm doing some work on a case and as my associate told you, was hoping to learn more about Adele and Gavin and their life here when she lived next door."

"Adele and Roger, her husband, moved in right after we did.

The houses, this whole development was brand new then. Roger was a probation officer, and Adele was a housewife and doted on little Gavin. We got together with them from time to time for dinner or cookouts. We had girls close to Gavin's age, so when they were young, they played together, but not as much when they were older."

She took a sip from her cup with a faraway look in her eyes. "We all just lived our lives and then when Roger died in that car accident, it was a real blow to poor Adele and Gavin. She took classes at the community college and did some temp work, I think, until she got a job working for that big amusement company in Nashville. She was intent on making sure Gavin could go to college and worked hard to find a good-paying job so she could make that happen."

"And she never remarried in all the years she lived here?" Coop asked.

Mrs. Davis shook her head. "No, she was focused on work and Gavin. I think she threw everything she had into him after Roger died. She would walk over hot coals for that boy to give him everything he desired. She didn't go to college, and I know it was hugely important to her that Gavin go. She wanted every opportunity and success for him and had to work extra hard with Roger gone."

She brought the cup to her lips and then set it down. "There was a man, a guy who worked with Roger, who came by quite often to take care of the yard and fix things around the house for her. I think he was sweet on her, but nothing ever came of it. She was so charming, with a wonderful smile, beautiful blonde hair, and such a petite woman. She had a way about her, sort of a helplessness, but she wasn't." The woman grinned. "I think she knew men liked to rescue women like her, you know?"

"Do you remember his name?"

Mrs. Davis stared out the window, her forehead creased. "It'll come to me." She tapped her fingers against the side of her mug. "I can picture him. He was devoted to her, and my husband and I thought for sure they'd get together, but it never happened."

"Did he work for the State of Tennessee or the county?"

"The state. He and Roger worked in the same office." She smacked her hand on the table. "Jerry Corman, that was his name." She grinned. "I told you it would come to me."

Coop jotted the name in his notebook. "That's a great help, thank you." Coop finished his coffee and let Mrs. Davis reminisce about the past, while she pointed at the photos of her family that hung on the wall.

She sighed and added, "I miss those days when the girls were young, and life was simpler. With my husband passing, I'm alone here for the most part, except for a visit from them a couple of times a year. They both live out of state and are busy with their families."

Coop's heart ached for the woman, who longed for company and conversation, but he didn't have time to dawdle. "I happen to live with my aunt, and she's close to your age. She fills her days with book clubs and garden clubs and spends some time at our community center. You might enjoy something like that." He took his empty cup to the sink. "I'm afraid I need to get back to the office, but you've been a great help, Mrs. Davis. Thank you for the coffee, too."

"Oh, you're more than welcome. A book club sounds like fun. I'll have to ask about one when I visit the library next time. If you think of anything else you need to know, I hope you'll come back and visit again."

She started to get up, but Coop put a hand on her shoulder. "You stay here and enjoy the rest of your coffee. I can see myself out. Thank you again."

Coop climbed behind the wheel of the Jeep and hurried back to the office. He found AB at her desk and asked her to start the research into Jerry Corman who worked for the Tennessee Department of Corrections when Adele lived in Murfreesboro.

While she queried the computer, Coop called Ben to see if he could check out Jerry and Adele's first husband through his channels. Coop was scanning old newspaper articles and AB was busy going through databases, when Gus darted from his chair to the back door.

"Dad and Aunt Camille must be here with lunch." Coop pushed back from the conference table and hurried to the parking lot to help them. Aunt Camille had packed enough food in the back of her car to feed the entire neighborhood.

As he used potholders to carry the heavy casserole dish, Coop recognized the aroma of his aunt's hot brown turkey casserole. He couldn't wait to dig into the cheesy and bacon goodness of it. After carting in the side dishes and a container of fresh cookies, Coop made sure everyone had a beverage and took his seat at the kitchen table.

While they ate, Coop told his aunt about Mrs. Davis and his conversation with her. "She's very nice but lonely, and she loves to read. I kept thinking one of the members of your book club lived in Murfreesboro. Don't you go there for a meeting sometimes?"

She nodded as she speared an apple in the fruit salad. "Yes, Ruby Faye lives out there and has for years." She winked at her nephew. "I see where you're going. Just give me her number, and I'll call her to talk her into joining us. She won't be able to refuse, I promise."

Coop grinned and nodded. "I knew I could count on you."

Charlie and Camille were headed to the community center for the rest of the afternoon and part of the evening. There was a pinochle tournament going on, and they were playing partners in it. "The more games we win, the later we'll be, so wish us luck," said Charlie with a grin.

Aunt Camille insisted Coop and AB keep the leftovers for lunch tomorrow and after Charlie nabbed another cookie, he and Camille made their way to the car. Coop watched them help each other down the steps and noticed his dad was walking better; the range of motion in his knee was improving each day.

He was relieved they had been able to convince him to recuperate in Nashville, and Coop was getting accustomed to having him around the house. Charlie, Coop thought, was enjoying himself and all the outings Aunt Camille foisted upon him. Coop wasn't looking forward to the day his dad would have to return to Nevada but knew it would be here soon.

After they cleaned up the kitchen, Coop and AB took a plate of cookies and went back to work at the conference table. Jerry still lived in Murfreesboro and had retired from the State of Tennessee, having worked as a probation officer his entire career. He had no children and had been divorced since he was in his thirties.

Nothing in his records stood out. He had a nice home, but nothing above his means. Other than working with Roger, had no other connection to Adele. Coop added his name and phone number to his notebook, intent on paying him a visit and seeing what he could tell him about Adele.

In the late afternoon, Ben called Coop back and confirmed most of the information Coop and AB had unearthed. "The guys I know didn't have much to say about him one way or the other. He was a career guy, retired, never rising too high in rank, and seemed content to put in his time. Nobody remembers a girlfriend or anything much about his personal life. I've got his address, phone, and cell numbers if you need them." Ben rattled them off, and Coop added the cell phone number to his notebook.

Late in the afternoon, Coop's excitement at learning about

Jerry had faded. Nothing they'd found shed any light on the case.

He was busy staring at the notes he'd written on the glass board when the rush of AB's footsteps outside his office door startled him. She came into the office, smiling. "I just got off the phone with Huck Grover. He apologized and said he was out of town and just returned home and checked his messages."

18

Huck was home from a family trip with his daughters and agreed to meet with Coop as soon as he could get there. AB reminded him to replace his t-shirt with one of the nice button-down company shirts he kept in his office. She wanted Huck to take him seriously, and the older generation appreciated a well-dressed professional.

Coop agreed and stuffed his DON'T WORRY WHAT OTHER PEOPLE THINK, THEY DON'T DO IT OFTEN t-shirt into the armoire and slipped into a black button down. He gave Gus, who was stationed at AB's desk, a quick pet and set out for Brentwood.

He pulled into Huck's driveway less than thirty minutes later and admired the immaculate brick colonial revival home with a manicured yard. Coop rang the bell, and a cheerful-looking man with a snowy white ring of hair circling his mostly bald head extended his hand. "You must be Mr. Harrington. Come on in."

"Call me Coop, please." Coop stepped through the double-door entry.

The man nodded. "You can call me Huck, and we'll go in

here. My wife's out at the store and running a few errands, but I've got some fresh coffee if you'd like to join me in a cup."

A man after his own heart, and what AB didn't know wouldn't hurt her. "I'd love it. Add a little sugar to mine if you don't mind."

Huck returned with two cups and took a seat on one of the dark leather sofas atop the wooden floor. "So, your colleague said you're looking into a case concerning Frank Covington."

"Right." Coop nodded as he swallowed a sip of the delicious brew. "It's a confidential matter, but I'm trying to learn more about Royal Amusement and specifically the period of time concerning the accidents before he sold the company and right around the time you left. From what I could tell, you had been there more than twenty years, right from the beginning."

Huck nodded, a faraway look in his eyes. "I started with Frank soon after I passed my exam to become an accountant. His company was growing, and he was a great idea guy but needed someone to handle the nuts and bolts and keep the books. We worked well together, and the company was quite successful. It was a great place to work... until it wasn't."

Huck paused in thought, and Coop sipped his coffee while he waited.

"Frank gave this young kid Gavin a chance and brought him on to work under me. He was fresh out of school with his MBA and thought he knew everything. Frank wanted me to show him the ropes and groom him to eventually take over the business side when I was ready to retire. Anyway, he had big ideas and pushed for more profits. That's all he wanted to see. He was into cutting expenses to boost profits. He put lots of pressure on the carnival bosses and tried to incentivize them with bonuses and such."

Coop nodded, interested. "Do you think that played into the accidents?"

Huck's eyes clouded and he nodded. "Sadly, yes, I do. I had

mentioned I was concerned about Gavin's tactics, but Frank told me not worry. I had to embrace the new ideas, and he wanted me to give Gavin a fair chance. After a couple of times mentioning I had some reservations about him and Frank shutting me down, I didn't bring it up again. It also complicated matters that Gavin was Adele's son."

He took a long swallow from his cup. "I didn't like Gavin or his new ideas. I had always presented Frank with the facts and would provide my opinion or ideas but left it to him. Gavin was intent on giving the company a new direction and after the accidents, I made up my mind that I'd look for something else. I was miserable and hated going to work. After Mrs. Covington died, Frank seemed even less interested in what I had to say. My wife and I decided as much as we hated the idea of moving, it would make our lives easier, so I had just given my notice when Frank's son died."

Coop scribbled on his notepad. "Tell me more about that time period. Did you know Dax?"

Huck smiled. "Dax was a good kid. He was in college and was devastated by his mother's death and the horrible accidents preceding it. He had been closer to his mom than Frank, I know. From what I gathered, he was trying to figure out what happened and posed as a carnival worker but ended up dying in a horrible fire when the division was in Georgia. Frank was shattered after that, and his head wasn't at work. After that, there was no point in me sticking around. I left a few days after the funeral."

"Some of the people I've talked to said you were a great business manager and knew how to keep the place profitable, always had your eye on expenses and wanted to keep them low. You mentioned Gavin had some new ideas about tying bonuses to profits. That seems like an incentive that might line up with your ideas, what did you think?"

Huck nodded. "I am all about keeping expenses low and

income high. That's the simple equation to profit, and I understand about tying bonuses to profit, but I had some reservations about the lengths some of our bosses would go to keep those numbers high, meaning cutting back on maintenance. That was an area that can't be sacrificed in that business. It was a matter of safety and ultimately could tarnish the brand to where it would implode. I thought there were other, less reckless ways of making sure our expenses stayed as low as possible."

"I understand you sent Gavin out to the sites to monitor their cash procedures and do spot checks. Do you remember if he was on such a visit when the fire occurred in Georgia?"

His forehead creased. "Mmm, you know, I do remember that he was out of the office only because some of the ladies were organizing meals for Frank and the kids, and Gavin wasn't there to sign up for a spot. Not that he would have. I'm sure Adele would have made sure to cover for him, but he wouldn't lift a finger to help anyone else. He was all about Gavin and climbing the ladder."

"Could he have been at Rex's division?"

Huck shook his head. "I doubt it. Rex ran our largest division and did an excellent job. He'd been there a long time, and we'd never had a problem. Honestly, I could tell by the numbers, I'd been doing it long enough to know when there should be a dip or a rise in cash receipts. I sent Gavin in the field just to get rid of him for the most part. His work didn't help me that much, and I hated to subject Rex to him. The trips made Gavin feel important, and that kept him happy."

"From what you're saying, it sounds like you and Frank got on well for years, but the addition of Gavin drove a wedge between the two of you. Is that accurate?"

Huck shrugged. "It wasn't something I whined to Frank about. It was just an unease I felt, and Adele made it awkward. I felt a bit pushed out, as she did all she could to help Gavin look like a shining star. More and more she seemed to circumvent my access to Frank, or I'd set up a meeting, and then he wouldn't be there, and she'd say it was a mistake. Frank put his trust in Adele, and they were close. It wouldn't have been wise to pit myself against her and her son. I saw the writing on the wall. It was easier just to leave."

Coop scribbled in his notebook. "This is going to sound odd, based on what you've told me, but did you ever direct the carnival bosses to skimp on maintenance and falsify the logs?"

Huck's smile disappeared, and he went pale. "Never. I would never do such a thing. My biggest fear was that the bonus scheme Gavin came up with would make them do something stupid like that. Gavin didn't run it by Frank, either. I think he was trying to impress him and show him he could do a better job than me."

"I've talked to Marvin and Frank about this, and they both deny telling the bosses to do that, but I've got a former worker who gave a statement and said that Rex had been told to do that."

Huck shook his head and sighed. "Marvin wouldn't have done that, and neither would Frank. It had to be Gavin. He was so intent on showing Frank his ideas could make more profit that he was willing to do anything. He wanted to push me out, I realize that now. Trust me, there wasn't much more we could do to make the profit margin higher. It was as high as I thought we could go, safely."

Coop asked about the process for the maintenance logs, and Huck confirmed that they were transmitted on paper, usually by fax or mail, and then the clerks would input the data into the computer system, and the software could provide reports. Huck set his cup on the coffee table. "Gavin knew there was no way my staff would have any part of monkeying with the records, so he went to the source. He probably used my name, or Frank's, to convey the new procedure."

He leaned back in his chair and stared at the ceiling for a

moment. "We were overboard on safety and maintenance, but we had a spotless record, and Frank wanted to keep it that way. Nobody wants to take their kid to a carnival where the machinery and rides look like they're falling apart. It sounds odd, but if you can imagine, we provided a high-end carnival experience, and that was one of the reasons for our success. Frank didn't tolerate shoddy workmanship and wanted the employees to look clean and wear matching shirts. He wanted it to be as professional as possible."

"Do you think Red Fulton from Big Top could have been involved in convincing someone, maybe Gavin, to sabotage the business from the inside, since he wanted to buy it?"

"Oh, boy. That's a pretty low maneuver. I can't imagine he would. Red did run a much looser operation, but I can't fathom him jeopardizing lives. He and Frank had a friendly competition. I can't see him doing that, but I honestly don't know."

Coop checked his notes. "Were you surprised when Frank and Adele married?"

His eyes widened. "Yes and no. Adele had a way of cozying up to men like Frank—rich, successful. I think it was no secret she admired him." He held up a hand. "Now, don't get me wrong. Frank didn't encourage it, and I never saw a hint of impropriety on his part. It was subtle in the way she behaved around him and fawned over him, especially after Laura Beth's death. So, I wasn't really surprised, but at the same time, I was shocked that Frank would remarry so soon after losing Dax. I'm not sure he was in a state to make such important decisions. He was completely devastated."

Coop rested his pen atop his notebook. "There's some new evidence that suggests the fire at the carnival site wasn't an accident, and Frank believes it was deliberate."

Huck shook his head. "Oh, my goodness. That's horrible news, just awful. Poor Frank, and I know he's not in the best of health. That's unbelievable."

"Dax called Frank the day before the fire and left him a message on his private answering machine. Do you have any knowledge of that call or message?"

Huck frowned. "No, not at all. Frank did have an answering machine on his desk, but I never used it or saw anyone use it but Frank and Adele."

"Would Gavin have had access to it?"

Huck nodded. "Sure, along with everyone else who worked in the office. Frank's office was rarely locked, and people were in and out of it all the time."

Coop took a quick sip of coffee. "Now, this won't sound very friendly, but I need to ask. The timing of your exit from the company drew my interest, being soon after the fire and not long after the slew of accidents. I have to say it raises suspicion."

Huck sighed and hung his head. "That's just horrible news about Dax, and I can see why my quick exit drew your attention. I'm not sure how to prove a negative, but I can assure you I had nothing to do with the fire, Dax's death, or the accidents. I was just tired of watching what we had built fall out from under us and couldn't stay. It impacted my happiness, and I wanted away from a family business. With all the good that came from it, there was an awful lot of dysfunction within, and it was too much for me."

Huck's shoulders sagged. "That sounds harsher than I wanted it to. Believe me, I went back and forth about my decision, feeling guilty for leaving Frank when he was in such a dark place, but the idea of having to work even closer with Gavin made the decision easy. I knew with Frank and Adele getting married, Gavin would only become more powerful. I couldn't take it, so I left."

Coop finished his coffee, and they visited for a few more minutes, but Huck didn't have anything to add. He hadn't seen Frank after he moved to Memphis. When he returned to the Nashville area, he never considered reconnecting. "That part of my life was long over. Now, I'm intent on enjoying my retirement with my wife and our grown daughters and grandchildren."

Coop left him with his business card and asked him to call if he remembered anything else about the time of the fire. He was careful not to divulge the news about Dax, even though it was bound to become public after the party Frank and Adele were hosting.

19

Friday morning, Ben was sitting in their booth when Coop arrived at Peg's, sporting a black t-shirt with white lettering—IN MY DEFENSE I WAS LEFT UNSUPERVISED. Myrtle chuckled when she saw it and poured his coffee, talking them into the apple-cinnamon pancakes. Ben slid a manila file folder across the table. "The initial dental comparison on the bones in Dax's grave are a match to this missing person."

Coop opened the file and saw a photo of a young man, smiling. He looked a bit like Dax, and the file showed his name as Jacob Nathan Harris. He was from Mississippi and had been reported missing several months after the fire. Seeing his face and knowing in his heart he had been murdered, Coop's appetite faded. "His poor family."

Ben nodded and swallowed a gulp of coffee. "I know. I hate these kinds of cases. We're going to hold off on a formal notification until we have the verified forensics, hopefully, this afternoon. In my gut, I'm sure it's him."

"Let me know when I can tell Frank and Dax. I know it's important to them."

Coop's cell phone chimed, and one glance at it showed AB

calling. He flicked the button on the screen. "Hey, AB. What's up? Do you have a breakfast request?"

He listened for a few moments and said, "Okay, I'll head over there as soon as we're done here."

He disconnected and took a long swallow from his cup. "So, yesterday, I talked to Huck Grover, the business manager who worked for Frank for years and left right after the RV fire. He called AB just now and said he wanted me to stop by. He remembered he kept a box of old records from his time at Royal and thought they might prove helpful."

"Maybe that will be the lucky break you need." Ben dug into his stack of pancakes topped with warm bits of apple topping laced with cinnamon and syrup to make a caramel-like sauce.

"I was convinced Huck must have had something to do with all of this, since he was a person in authority at Royal and, from what Gavin said, stressed the profitability angle, which could have led to the skimping on maintenance and the accidents. After talking to him, I don't think he was involved and now with him calling and offering his records, I'm even more sure he's got nothing to do with it. He seems like a nice guy who had enough of working in a family business and just wanted out. I think he knew the business would implode eventually."

"I'm sure you're right, but if I know you, you'll have AB going over his records with a fine-tooth comb to make sure of it."

Coop grinned at his old friend. "Already on it." He made quick work of breakfast, anxious to get to Huck's. Ben offered to drop AB's breakfast to her, so Coop could get on the road to Brentwood. Gus loved to go for a ride and sat in the passenger seat, his head swiveling as he took in everything along the way.

Coop made sure the windows were cracked down, so Gus would have all the fresh air he needed and hurried to the door. Huck greeted him with a smile and pointed to a banker's box that had yellowed with age. "After you left last night, I just kept thinking back to that time and remembered I took copies of a few things and kept them, worried specifically about those lawsuits that were being filed and anyone trying to implicate me or my staff in it. I'm not sure there will be anything helpful, but the one thing I did find is an expense report from Gavin that showed he was outside of Chattanooga the day of the fire. That puts him just over an hour from the site in Georgia."

"That's very helpful. I'll take it to the office and go through it, if that's okay with you."

Huck nodded. "Sure, I don't need any of it back. I had a bad feeling when I left, and it made me feel more secure to keep hold of it. I hope it helps."

Coop thanked him again and toted the box to the Jeep. Under the watchful eye of Gus, he put it in the backseat, and they headed back to the office.

Fortified with decaf, which was like eating Chinese and expecting to be full hours later, he dug into the box, going through the folders and papers. The expense report Huck mentioned was on top of the pile.

There were folders that contained copies of the maintenance reports at each site, income and expenses, including some detailed copies of bills that had been paid, and employee timesheets, which could prove helpful in locating anyone else that had been working at Royal at the time of the fire. It looked like he had a little bit of everything stuffed in the box, including his calendar for the year.

Coop and AB read through the papers, hoping something would spark an idea. The timesheets helped them identify all the employees at the office and the names of the carnival bosses at the sites of the accidents. A cursory look online showed that like Rex, they were also deceased.

The hours ticked by and before they knew it, it was time to close for the day and get ready for the party at the Covingtons.

AB offered to drive and promised to pick Coop up in less than an hour.

Coop discarded his t-shirt and after a quick shower, selected a jacket and green button-down shirt that AB always said was a favorite of hers, but couldn't bring himself to wear a tie. He made sure he had his cell phone and slipped his notepad into the inside jacket pocket just in case he ran across something important.

He ruffled Gus' ears and said goodbye to Aunt Camille and his dad, who were having a casual supper in the kitchen, still basking from their third-place win in the tournament yesterday. They had won gift cards to a local coffee spot known for their homemade pies, and the two made plans to use them on the weekend.

Coop's heart swelled seeing how much happier Aunt Camille was since Charlie had come to stay with them. He gave her a purpose, and she forced him to socialize, which despite his initial resistance, Coop could tell his dad actually enjoyed the time.

He scooted out the door and climbed into the passenger seat of AB's waiting VW Bug. Each time he sat in it, he felt like his knees were folded to his chin, but it was a short trip down the road. AB wore dress pants and that same shimmery sweater she wore when they went to Houston's. She handed him the beautifully wrapped box she had moved to allow him to sit.

"Oh, nice. What did we get Lindsay for her birthday?"

"A lovely leather journal engraved with her name." AB shrugged. "It's my go-to gift when I don't know the person well enough to pick something else."

"Sounds perfect and classy." Coop's phone chimed, and he saw a text from Ben. "Ah, Ben says they just received the official confirmation on the remains. It's definitely Jacob Nathan Harris. We can let Frank know."

Minutes later, they arrived at the large estate and agreed she should park along the edge of the street rather than get trapped in the sweeping driveway. Coop gestured to a good spot. "I don't want to stay long, so we can sneak out and leave without having to deal with cars boxing us in."

As they walked across the expanse, AB gestured to the cars. "I didn't expect this many people."

As they reached the steps to the front door, soft piano music filtered from inside the house. A young woman dressed in a black catering uniform opened the door and welcomed them inside. She offered to take their coats and placed their gift on a table overflowing with packages, before she directed them through the entry to the huge living room, where the hum of conversation filled the space and echoed off the high ceiling. Fresh flower bouquets decorated the space, along with thousands of twinkling lights strung along the balcony above and outside on the large patio visible off the glass doors. They even had portable heaters outside to make sure their guests were comfortable in the space.

It didn't take long for Lindsay to notice them, and she strode across the space to welcome them. She was the belle of the ball in her deep-blue gown that matched her eyes and looked stunning with her dark hair. "Thanks for coming. It means so much to Dad and Dax... and me."

Coop extended his hand and offered birthday wishes. AB hugged her. "Happy Birthday, Lindsay. I imagine it's surreal to have Dax here with you this year."

She smiled and nodded with enthusiasm. "It's the best birthday I've had in a very long time. It's been great for Dad, too. He's got a new outlook, even with his diagnosis."

Coop gestured to Frank, who was across the room with his arm around Dax. "He was so excited to have this gathering to honor your birthday and Dax's homecoming. It's great to see him and Dax together."

Lindsay smiled at the two of them and then turned her

attention to Coop and AB. "Are you any closer to figuring out what happened?"

Coop's brow furrowed. "The police just received a confirmation on the identification of the remains. They're notifying his family tonight. As far as who might have been behind the fire or the accidents, we're making some progress, but nothing concrete yet."

Lindsay brought her hand to her chest. "That's horrible for his family. I know Dad and Dax are really upset by it. I'm trying to stay focused on the blessing of having my brother back home." She led them to the large kitchen area with buffet tables piled with food. Catering staff moved through the house with flutes of champagne and a host of other offerings.

"Please help yourself to something to eat. I'm told there is a birthday cake that will be unveiled later in the evening. It's my favorite, a chocolate layer cake filled with a mocha mousse and covered with chocolate fudge frosting." Her eyes sparkled when she described it.

Coop's eyebrows arched. "You had me at chocolate."

Lindsay laughed and waved at a couple who was just coming through the entryway. "I'll leave you two to mingle. Thanks again for coming."

AB watched her walk over and hug the older couple. "She's a sweet person. Not like most women her age born into such wealth. She's quite genuine."

Coop nodded. "Hopefully, with Dax back home, it will help her anxiety. It would have been tough for her when Frank eventually passes. She'd be alone, and I think Gavin and Adele could definitely overrun her."

They filled their plates with the heavy appetizers and found a seat in the family room, where Coop had met Adele earlier in the week. It was off the beaten path, and they were the only two occupants, making it easy for them to observe the festivities. Coop recognized several people from the various soirees he had attended with Aunt Camille over the years. Like most of her generation that had lived in Belle Meade for years, she was dialed into the prevalent, posh happenings in their circles.

Adele was in her element, floating through the guests in an elegant pink chiffon pantsuit embellished with embroidery and glittery beads on the cuffs and neckline. She smiled and laughed with each group, taking care to make sure Lindsay visited with everyone. All the witnesses Coop had interviewed described Adele as charming, and she was every bit the engaging hostess.

On one of her trips through the kitchen where she looked over the shoulder of the caterers and made sure things were running smoothly, she spied Coop and AB. After making sure more of the popular pork sliders were put out, she made a beeline for them. "Lovely to see you two here tonight. Lindsay said she chatted with you earlier."

Coop stood. "Thank you for having us. You've outdone yourself. It's a wonderful evening. Lindsay is excited about her cake, and Frank looks terrific tonight."

She batted her eyelashes at the compliment and then glanced across the expanse, her eyes scanning the space until they found Frank. "I do hope he's not overdoing it. I worry about him getting too tired."

AB smiled and said, "I think he looks great and so very happy. It's wonderful that he has this time with Dax and Lindsay."

"Oh, yes. He hasn't spent more than a few hours apart from Dax since his return." Coop stared at her happy smile but picked up on the slight irritation in her tone.

Coop gestured at the two of them, Frank with his arm around his son as he introduced him to another couple of friends. "I'm sure they're both just trying to make up for lost time. It's not easy to cram in twenty-five years' worth of memories and experiences in such a short time."

"Well, that certainly isn't Frank's fault, is it?" She turned her head at the sound of glass breaking. She rolled her eyes and added, "I best check on that. It's hard to get good help these days."

With a flutter of chiffon, she made her exit to the kitchen.

Coop returned to his seat and his plate of food. AB's eyes lingered as she took in Adele giving one of the catering staff a tongue lashing. "I wonder if Dax has picked up on her animosity toward him. She sure is reluctant to cut him any slack."

"I can't imagine her hiding it. She and Gavin seem to be the only people in Frank's orbit who aren't celebrating Dax's return." Coop dipped his head in the other direction where Gavin was leaning against one of the columns between the entryway and the living space, a scowl on his face.

Coop wiped his mouth with a napkin and took a swallow from his glass of iced tea. "Might as well let Gavin know we have an expense report that shows where he was the day of the fire. Maybe he'll remember something."

AB smiled. "I doubt it will improve his mood. I'll stay here and keep an eye on the crowd."

Coop made his way over to Gavin. "Enjoying the party?" he asked.

Gavin shrugged and took a healthy sip of champagne. "I'm not staying long. Just making an appearance on my way home from work. I told Mom I had plans, but she insisted I stop by. Told me it wouldn't be proper to skip it."

Coop put his hand on Gavin's shoulder. "Well, I'm glad you're here. I found some old files today, and an interesting expense report you filed shows you were outside of Chattanooga on the day of the fire at the carnival site. Does that ring a bell?"

Gavin smirked. "Not really, but you are thorough. I'll give you that. Like I told you before, I've been all over Tennessee for Huck's stupid inspections."

"Right," said Coop. "I just thought it could nudge your

memory since it was so close to the site in Georgia and might help you remember something. It's only about what, an hour away from the site?"

Gavin shook his head. "Still not jogging any memories. Dax's death didn't rank high on my list of memorable events. Sure, I felt bad for Frank, but I was young and focused on my own stuff. It didn't have that big of an impact."

Coop looked across the room at Frank laughing and patting his son on the back. "Well, his return is something I'm sure you'll remember. It's probably more meaningful for you. Now that you're older and all, right?"

Gavin's eyes narrowed as he stared at Coop. "I'm already late and need to say goodbye to Mom. Enjoy the rest of your evening." He sauntered away in the direction of Adele.

Coop started to walk back toward AB when Dax put a hand on his arm. "Hey, Mr. Harrington. I saw you and AB earlier but didn't get a chance to say hello. Thanks for coming."

"AB and I were just saying how happy your dad looks. It's great to see."

He grinned as he watched his dad. "Yeah, it's been a crazy couple of weeks, and I still can't believe I'm here. Being with Lindsay, especially for her birthday, and Dad has made me so grateful. I know Dad's diagnosis is grim, but he's agreed to visit with an alternative medicine specialist and see what he says. I kick myself that I wasted all this time because I wasn't brave enough to reach out." He glanced at the floor. "I could have figured out a way to do it and even remained in England. It was just something that was too hard for me to face, I think."

"That's understandable. What's important is that you're here for your dad and Lindsay now."

"Any new developments?"

Coop sighed. "The police identified the young man's remains. His name was Jacob Nathan Harris, and he was from Mississippi."

Dax sighed and shook his head. "I feel so guilty for his death. I know Dad wants to reach out to his family and try to do something for them. I'm not sure it's a great idea, but I understand the sentiment and his intentions."

Coop gritted his teeth. "It might be best to wait a bit and let them come to terms with the news."

"Let me tell Dad. I don't want to ruin his high spirits tonight."

Coop nodded. "I met with Huck yesterday. He's been out of town and called me when he returned. I was counting on him to be the primary suspect, but after talking with him, I don't think he had anything to do with it. He kept some old records from Royal and among those, we found an expense claim from Gavin for the day of the fire. He was outside of Chattanooga."

Dax's eyes widened. "Wow. That puts him close to the area. He's been pretty distant since I returned. I don't think he's as happy to see me as Lindsay and Dad are."

"Did you know each other from before, when Adele worked for your dad?"

"Not really. I'd met him, but we didn't actually know each other. Adele brought him to events when Royal had family parties and picnics, but that's the only time I ever saw him. I think he went to college in Knoxville."

Coop nodded. "That's right. He just seems to have a chip on his shoulder when it comes to you."

"I think Dad looked upon him as a son and now that I'm back, Gavin probably feels like an outsider. I have a feeling when he learns about Dad's new instructions for the estate, he'll be even more unhappy."

"There's a good chance that news could be met with resentment. I take it your dad hasn't said anything yet?"

Dax shrugged. "I don't think so. He was looking forward to this party, and I'm sure he didn't want to create any angst before it. I suspect he'll share the news next week."

Coop's eyes drifted to Gavin as he strode to the door and made his exit. "Hopefully, it won't be too stressful for your dad. I haven't shared the expense report information with him and would rather wait until next week, so as not to put a damper on the party, like you suggested."

"I'm pretty protective of him, but at this point, I'm not sure much will ruffle him. He's so happy to have me home and have Lindsay and me together, I think he's impervious to anything else."

"Let's hope so," said Coop.

The tinkling sound of a spoon on a champagne flute interrupted their conversation. Everyone turned their attention to Frank, who stood with Lindsay in front of the glass doors that led out to the patio, where people came in from the outdoors. Dax shook Coop's hand. "That's my signal. I better join them."

Coop found his way back to AB, and they stood on the edge of the living area where they had a view of the guests and the makeshift stage where Dax and Lindsay flanked Frank.

Frank cleared his throat, and his eyes swept the room. "Where's Adele?" Moments later, she came from the entryway and hurried across the room. She slipped in between Frank and Lindsay and put an arm around the birthday girl.

"We want to thank you all for coming to celebrate with us tonight. Not only is it my lovely daughter Lindsay's birthday, but we're also thrilled to be able to welcome Dax, my son, home. As I've visited with all of you here tonight, you've learned the story about what happened so long ago and rather than spend any time rehashing the past tonight, I'm just thankful Dax is home and looking forward to the future and the time I can spend with him and Lindsay."

He turned to Adele and smiled. "My heartfelt thanks to my lovely wife Adele, for putting together a wonderful evening and for her support over the last twenty-five years. Let's all raise a glass to Lindsay, and then we'll sing to her and have a piece of this delicious cake I've been hearing about all day."

The guests raised their glasses and showered Lindsay with love and birthday wishes. Adele kissed her cheek and hugged her. The caterers rolled out the cake on a wheeled stand, while the guests gasped at the glowing confection decorated with several sparklers. After everyone sang to Lindsay, she cut the first piece of cake and presented it to her brother.

An older gentleman standing near Frank tapped his glass and looked around the room, waiting for the guests to quiet down. "For those of you who don't know me, I'm Ed, one of Frank's oldest friends, and I can't let the evening go by without raising our glasses to Dax. It's nothing short of a miracle and a dream come true to see him back home with his dad and Lindsay. I've never seen Frank this happy or looking so great. Join me in toasting Dax."

The guests raised their glasses and burst into applause. Dax stepped forward after the noise subsided. "Thank you, Ed. I'm the luckiest guy in the room tonight and am beyond thrilled to be back here in Nashville with my dad and Lindsay. Like Ed said, it's a dream come true. I'm sorry it took so long, but I'm so happy to be here with them now. Thank you for coming and happiest of birthdays to my little sister."

As the catering staff passed out slices to all the guests, Coop took his first bite and moaned with delight at the mingling of chocolate and coffee. He kept his eye on the guests and the family. Everyone in the room was smiling, some even wiping away emotional tears at the sight of Dax hugging his dad and sister. Everyone that is, except Adele.

20

After the excitement of the cake and toasts and more mingling, Frank sought out AB and Coop and sat with them in the family room. "I'm thrilled you both came tonight. It was fitting that the two people who helped bring my son back to me joined in our celebration."

Guests gathered their coats and left, with Dax and Lindsay on hand to say goodbye to them. After taking a bite of his slice of cake, Frank looked behind him at the kitchen and then lowered his voice. "Dax said you met up with Huck. Was he any help?"

Coop nodded and filled him in on the visit he had with Huck. "He seems like a genuine guy. We'll dig into his life a bit deeper, but as much as I was hoping he was behind the maintenance scam, I honestly don't think he had anything to do with it. He wanted me to pass on his best to you. He told me much of the reason he left was because of Gavin and the feeling he had that the company was in jeopardy after the accidents. He wanted to avoid that drama."

Frank's smile faded a bit. "I can understand that and can't say that I blame him. Gavin had lots of ideas but wasn't the best at communicating them or valuing the history of the company and all Huck had done to help build that business. I should have seen it coming, but I wasn't operating at my best in those days, especially not after losing Laura Beth."

Coop took a deep breath. "We're not giving up and are still following up on some leads. I've got some theories. Maybe we can talk more next week. Tonight, just enjoy your family and the party."

Moments later, Dax came around the corner. "Dad, Ed and his wife want to see you before they leave."

"Yes, of course. I'll be right there."

Coop met Frank's eyes. "How about we meet at the office and discuss this in more detail this weekend or Monday?"

Frank stood and nodded. "That's a good idea. I'd like to get my head around it. Monday afternoon, Dax and Lindsay are taking me to a new doctor, so maybe we could do it Monday morning?"

"Works for us," said Coop. "It was a lovely party, and I agree with Lindsay, this cake is over-the-top delicious."

Frank smiled again and waved to them as he made his way to the entryway.

The caterers were clearing out, toting their boxes out through a side door that led to the rear driveway where their vehicles were parked. Coop bent to grab several napkins that had fallen out and hurried to catch up to the woman. The evening was nice and instead of returning to the kitchen, he walked around the house, hoping to capture a glimpse of the patio decorated with the twinkle lights from a different vantage point.

The backyard was a stunning expanse of lawn and mani-cured shrubbery with planters, lit by soft lights. During spring and summer, it had to be breathtaking. As Coop suspected, the patio was much prettier from the outside. He made his way up the steps and under the covering and was about to reach for the door when he heard a voice above him.

He moved to the edge of the patio, still under the canopy and when he recognized Adele's voice, tilted his head to listen.

"Frank told me this morning that he's making a change to his estate. He didn't come right out and say it, but I know with Dax back, things are going to change and not to my benefit. I need Frank gone before he can do that and leave me with nothing."

There was a lull, and Adele was silent for almost a minute. Coop realized she must be on the phone.

"Listen, last time you helped me, it was for Gavin, not me. This time, it's for me. It needs to look like an accident, and it needs to happen soon. I overheard Frank talking to that interfering detective, who's also a lawyer. Frank's going to see him Monday morning, and I'm sure he's going to ask him to handle the estate."

After a long pause, Adele's voice took on a new, sinister tone. "Don't threaten me. Remember, I know plenty about you and your past. Trust me, this is the last time, and I'll make it worth your while. Once this is done, I'll have plenty of money to share."

At the sound of her heels above, Coop could picture her pacing the balcony.

She laughed, almost purring. "We'll see about that. I'll need to grieve properly, you know."

After a few moments of silence, she spat out one more instruction. "I don't want to know anything about it. Just get one of your lowlife minions to handle it like you did last time, but make sure they do it right. I trusted you to take care of things twenty-five years ago, and you made a mess of it. No mistakes this time."

The heavy tap of her heels disappeared, and the click of a door closing prompted Coop to hurry around the house and back to the side door of the kitchen. He came through the door and saw Lindsay and Dax visiting with AB, a stack of old photo albums spread on the counter.

Lindsay was having another piece of cake and offered Coop a second helping. He shook his head. "I'd love to, but I'm stuffed. The food was fabulous."

She left her plate and walked across the kitchen to a stack of boxes and selected a large one. Then, she cut off a slab of cake, wide enough for several servings. "I insist you take some home and enjoy it. We have plenty."

AB grinned. "Coop never turns down free dessert."

Frank joined them a few minutes later, having stood outside visiting with Ed and his wife. He clapped his hands together. "What a great night, huh?" He hugged Lindsay. "Such a special birthday for my girl."

Adele came around the corner and surveyed the space, her eyes narrowing at the trail of crumbs on the counter. "Well, it looks like the caterer doesn't understand the meaning of leaving the kitchen clean."

Lindsay held up her hand. "That was me. I just cut a piece of cake for Mr. Harrington to take home and didn't have time to wipe it up yet."

Adele's eyes softened. "Oh, that's okay, sweetie. I'm just rattled because one of them broke a vase I had on the counter." She sighed. "It's been a long day, and I'm a bit worn out."

Frank reached out a hand to his wife. "Why don't you go on up to bed, dear? I'm still too excited, and the kids and I are going to look through these old albums."

Coop caught Adele's eye. "It was a fabulous event. Thanks again for having us. The food, especially the cake, was superb."

She beamed at the kind compliment. It was enough to soothe her earlier harshness. "I wanted Lindsay to have a perfect birthday and of course celebrate the excitement of Dax's homecoming. Overall, I think it was quite the success." She glanced up toward Frank. "I just don't want you getting over-tired. You'll have plenty of time to look at those old photos tomorrow."

Frank put his arm around her shoulder. "Am I the luckiest guy in the world, or what? Thank you again, my dear, for putting together the perfect evening."

Coop caught Dax's eye and gestured toward the door. "Well, we've stayed too late and need to get going."

AB added her thanks as they meandered toward the entry-way, and Lindsay retrieved their coats for them.

Dax moved from around the counter. "I'll walk you out."

AB led the way down the driveway. "We're parked on the street."

When they reached the edge of the property, Coop looked behind them and stopped walking. "Dax, I don't want to alarm you or your dad, but I overheard a conversation tonight that leads me to believe your life or your dad's life or maybe both are in jeopardy."

He quickly explained Adele's phone conversation. "I'm going to get in touch with the police tonight and see if they can do anything. Whoever she was talking to was involved in what happened twenty-five years ago. She knows your dad is coming to the office Monday morning, and she thinks he hasn't made any adjustments to the estate yet."

Dax shook his head. "This is unbelievable. This is going to devastate Dad."

"I know. I don't think you should tell him or Lindsay yet. I don't want either of them to act differently or give away the fact we know something is up. At the same time, we need to make sure you and your dad are safe."

Dax sighed. "I'll come up with something to get the three of us out of the house tomorrow morning, and we'll come to your office."

Coop nodded. "That's perfect. AB and I will get to work on

this tonight and try to identify the person on the other end of that call. Adele said she didn't want to know what was going to happen or be anywhere near it. That tells me whatever is planned, it probably won't happen at the house, but we can't be too careful."

"It's going to take every fiber in my being to not haul off and coldcock her. I can't believe she's involved. I thought she was just angry at me for causing Dad so much pain over the years."

AB looked back at the house. "Adele appears to have a genuine affection for Lindsay. Do you see that?"

Dax nodded. "Yes, she's doted on her since she married Dad. She's very kind and gentle with her and always concerned about her. I think Lindsay finds it stifling, especially now as an adult, but she's too sweet to say anything."

Coop stepped toward AB's car. "It's best that you get back inside and act normal. We don't need them wondering why you're out here so long. Keep your phone on vibrate, and I'll call you with any news we get tonight. I'd feel better if you text me every hour or so just to check in."

Dax nodded. "Will do. Thanks for looking out for us." He hurried back across the driveway while AB started the ignition and turned back toward Aunt Camille's.

"Shall I just go to the office?" she asked when they neared the turn for the house.

Coop nodded. "Yeah, let's get a game plan together."

21

C oop brewed a pot of coffee, and AB didn't give him the side eye when he filled the filter with real coffee. It would be a long night.

Coop put in a quick call to Aunt Camille to let her know they were working late, so she wouldn't worry. AB came through the door carrying two steaming cups of coffee and took a chair at the conference table.

Coop took a sip and pointed at his cell phone. "I wonder if Dax could get access to Adele's cell phone. I'm sure it's on the plan with the company, and I know you can get online and bring up our call histories for our lines."

AB nodded. "I'm sure he can, if he can get the password. It might be tricky since I'm sure Gavin handles that at the insurance office."

"I'm not sure Ben will have any luck getting a warrant, especially quickly, based on what I overheard." He picked up his cell phone and texted Dax. "If Dax can get the information, I asked him to get it to you, and we can get online and search for it."

AB nodded. "Whoever it is, he or she was in Adele's life twenty-five years ago. I don't think it's anyone who worked at

Royal. We've talked to everyone who was in a leadership position, and there's nothing to link them to the fire."

Coop tapped a message into his phone. "I'm texting Ben to let him know about the threat and what I heard. Maybe he can put somebody on the house to watch it through the weekend."

As soon as he pressed send, Coop's phone buzzed with a new message. He read through it and turned to AB. "Dax says he doesn't know the password but has keys to the insurance office and gave me the alarm code. He's going to slip outside and leave the keys on the pillar at the end of the driveway.

Coop slogged down a few gulps from his cup, and he and AB headed back to the Covington estate. AB slowed down and let Coop out a few yards before she reached the edge of the property. He jogged to the pillar, where he found a keyring next to the light on top of it.

He palmed the keys and hurried back to the waiting car. AB made a U-turn and drove to the insurance office. AB parked around the back of the building. The alarm code worked like a charm, and Coop locked the door behind them. They didn't use the lights in the office and made their way down the hallway to Gavin's office.

Coop took a small flashlight from his pocket and scanned the office. No file cabinets, but he saw a huge bank of them in Gavin's assistant's office, next door. He and AB moved to it and scanned the labels. AB whispered, "Here, I think it should be in this one." She shined the flashlight on the lock and read off the number. Coop found the corresponding file key on the ring.

Moments later, they had it opened and rifled through the hanging folders. AB found the file for the cellular provider and flipped through the agreements and bills until she found the information. "Gavin's assistant is very organized. Here's all the information we need." AB took a picture of the document with her phone and then replaced all the papers, so they were neat and in the same order she had found them.

They relocked the cabinet and made their way out of the office. As they came to the end of the hallway, Coop's arm shot out to his side, stopping AB from moving forward. Headlights flashed across the windows as a car pulled into the parking lot.

The office didn't share a parking lot with any other businesses. Coop stepped toward the front and squinted, trying to make out the shape of the vehicle. He whispered, "Let's go back and take cover in the conference room."

They hurried to the room and stood in a dark corner. They waited for the sound of the door unlocking, but after several minutes, were left in complete silence. Coop tiptoed down the hallway for a look. There was now another car parked next to the first one, and two people leaned against the vehicles, talking.

He let out a breath and went back to the conference room. "It was nobody. Just a couple of people parked and talking."

AB nodded. "Let's get out of here, then. We can leave from the side street, so they don't see us."

Coop punched in the alarm code again to reset the security system, and they locked the door behind them, waiting a few minutes to make sure no alarms sounded. AB had the car running, and he slid into the passenger seat.

She drove back to the Covington estate so Coop could replace the keys. Once they were back at the office, Coop warmed up their coffees, and AB set about logging into the Covingtons' cell phone account. She scrolled through until she found Adele's line and then dug into her call history. Coop stood behind her and watched.

"She only made one call during the party." AB scribbled down the number and handed it to him.

He nodded. "That has to be it, the time matches."

"I'll dig around and see if I can find it through our search tool. If I don't have any luck, you might have to call Ben and see if he can help."

Coop reached for his phone. "I put it on silent while we were breaking into the insurance office." He looked at the screen and nodded. "Missed a call from Ben."

"Technically, we had a key, so we weren't breaking in."

Coop grinned as he scrolled to his contacts. "You are correct, AB. Hey, just out of curiosity can you search the phone history on Adele's phone or any phone on their account to see if that number has been called before and when?"

AB's keys flew over the keyboard. "Already on it."

Coop's conversation with Ben was short. He disconnected his call and leaned against AB's desk. "Ben said if we don't find anything, send him the number, and he's going to put somebody on the Covington house. He wants Dax and Frank to stay together, so they don't have to spend extra manpower watching both of them."

While he talked, he texted Dax to let him know the keys had been returned and asked him to stay with Frank for the duration of the weekend to make it easier for the police to monitor them.

AB shook her head and turned from the screen. "I can only go back eighteen months, and that number isn't in the history of any phone on the account."

Coop eyed the paper with the number on it.

AB pointed at her screen. "The prefix tells me it's a wireless number based out of Murfreesboro."

"Back to Murfreesboro, where Adele lived all those years ago." Coop headed back to his office.

He turned on the glass whiteboard and scanned the list of names he had collected. Roger Pierce had been Adele's husband, and Jerry Corman was the friend Mrs. Davis said had worked with him and helped Adele after Roger's death.

Coop turned to his notebook and flipped back a few pages. He found what he was looking for and said, "Gotcha."

AB came through the door of Coop's office, smiling. "Our trusty search tool spit out a name."

Coop grinned. "Let me guess...Jerry Corman?"

AB shook her head. "Why do we pay for that expensive service when we have you?"

He chuckled. "Now that we have a name, run him through the system, and let's get a complete dossier on him."

Coop stared at the glass whiteboard and said, "I don't want to tip him off. I'll let Ben know he's our guy and see if he can bring him in based on me signing an affidavit about what I heard. I don't want to give Jerry any time to talk to Adele and concoct a story."

AB nodded. "Not to mention, we need to move quickly before he does anything to harm Frank or Dax."

22

Thankful that Ben was used to getting calls at all hours, Coop had called him late last night with Jerry Corman's name. They planned to gather as much information as they could and meet first thing Saturday morning at Coop's office, which was why Coop found himself at The Donut Hole at five o'clock in the morning. At least he had first pick of the fresh-from-the-oven creations.

Coop had taken care to pick his t-shirt of the day, and the woman behind the counter told him she loved the quote above the colorful donut-EAT MORE HOLE FOODS.

He toted the box to the Jeep, where Gus was waiting to give it a good sniff. Coop started a pot of coffee brewing and took one of the maple bacon donuts he loved from the box. He perused the file AB had prepared on Mr. Corman once more.

After one marriage that lasted less than a year, Corman had been divorced for over forty years. No children. Retired from his job as a probation officer and still living in Murfreesboro, albeit in a larger house. He volunteers as a mentor to parolees. Good credit rating, drives a new car, and likes to frequent restaurants and bars. Does a fair amount of traveling and has a modest amount of savings, deriving his income from his state pension. No criminal record, no traffic violations. Has a concealed carry permit.

Gus jumped from his chair and hurried down the hallway. That meant AB or Ben or both of them had arrived. Ben's deep voice drifted through the office, followed by AB greeting Gus with her usual sweet tone.

Minutes later, they both came into Coop's office with AB setting his steaming cup of coffee in front of him. Coop gestured to the pink bakery box. "Help yourselves, and then we'll get down to it."

Ben took out a sheet of paper from the file he carried and slid it across the conference table. "So, I used your sworn affidavit about Adele's call you overheard, plus what you added about your investigation, and I was able to get a pen register on Corman's phone. After Adele called, he made a call to one Levi, also known as Butch, Jennings."

Ben handed Coop another paper. "Butch is no stranger to law enforcement. He's been in jail, did a stint in prison, and you'll never guess who his probation officer was." He took a couple of bites from his donut while he gave Coop time to read.

"Since Butch is currently on probation, Kate and Jimmy paid him a visit and picked him up last night."

AB's eyebrows rose as she tore off bits of a blueberry donut. "Do tell."

Ben smiled as he chewed on the last bite of the raspberry jelly donut he favored. "It didn't take much to get him to sing like the proverbial canary. Butch told them he'd had a working relationship with Jerry Corman since his first time on probation when he was just nineteen years old."

Ben explained that Jerry had helped Butch out by being lenient with him and providing good reports, helping him avoid harsher sentencing in return for a few favors. If Butch showed any hesitation, Corman threatened to make his life tougher.

"They had him jabbering about all sorts of illegal activity over the last twenty-five years, and he gave them several details about a few other parolees who also worked for Corman. Then they brought out the file on the RV fire at the carnival. He confessed to knocking out the young man he thought was Dax and blowing out the pilot light, letting the trailer fill with gas, and then tossing in a cigarette on his way out the door. Says he was messed up on drugs at the time and wasn't in his right mind and scared of going to prison. He's spilling everything he knows, hoping for a deal."

Coop drummed his fingers on the paperwork from Ben. "So, we've got Corman, but now we need to connect him to Adele."

Ben nodded. "That's going to take a bit more finesse."

Coop's fingers quit moving. "Is Butch stable enough to have him make contact with Corman and wear a wire?"

Ben shrugged. "He's jumpy, but that's what we're thinking. I think if we brought Corman in, he'd lawyer up, and that would be the end of the conversation. He knows the system."

"If he's jumpy, that might be a good reason to have him call Corman and set up a meeting. He can tell him he's not sure about doing the job. Did Corman tell him what to do?"

Ben sighed. "Butch says he told him he needed to make it look like an accident, and it needs to happen before Monday morning, but no specifics."

Coop nodded. "I think we can use that to our advantage. Butch can say he's unsure and then press Corman for help on what he should do, exactly."

Ben scooped up the file folder he brought with him. "That's what Kate and Jimmy think, too. We're going to prep him and set something up for this morning. We need to move quickly so Corman doesn't get suspicious. Kate and Jimmy are catching some sleep while we let Butch rest. We want him as calm as possible."

Coop glanced at his watch. "We've got Frank, Dax, and Lindsay coming in first thing this morning."

Ben slipped one more donut into a stack of napkins and headed for the door. "I'll keep you posted and with any luck, we'll have Corman in the box before lunch."

Coop and AB cleaned up his office and conference table, so they'd be ready for their clients when they arrived. While he waited, Coop scrolled through his emails. He cocked his head when he saw one from Darcy Flint.

He opened it and read through it, his fists and jaw clenched. AB looked up from using a cloth to polish the wooden table and said, "Uh, oh. What's wrong?"

"In a word. Marlene."

She slipped into the chair in front of his desk. "Now what?"

"Ms. Flint said Marlene didn't show up at the senior center yesterday for her shift. She wanted to give her until today and went by the motel to check on her last night. The manager said she checked out yesterday morning."

"I wonder if she went back to Ruben's?"

Coop sighed. "Ms. Flint thought the same thing and checked at his place, but nobody was there."

"So, she's flown the coop?"

"It would seem that way. Now, she'll have a warrant out for her arrest."

"She's exasperating. I don't understand why she makes things so much harder than they need to be."

"She loves problems. Being one, making one, whatever. I think she thrives on the drama." He sat back in his chair, his hands behind his head. "I guess the upside is I cannot communicate with a known fugitive and will be forced to turn her into law enforcement should she make contact with me. So, if she calls, don't accept the charges. I'm done with her shenanigans."

∾

Coop slipped a sweatshirt with the firm's logo over his t-shirt and took Gus for a quick walk around the block to clear his head. He took pride in solving challenging problems, and his mother was one such dilemma that he would never be able to resolve. Years ago, he had tried a kinder and softer approach, but all that led to was more grief.

He only heard from her when she was in trouble and needed his help or his money. It was a dysfunctional relationship at best. He often wrestled with his feelings about his mother. She had broken his heart too many times to count and had been horrible to his father. Yet something deep inside him longed for her to change and be the loving mother he remembered from his childhood.

Maybe it had all been a façade. Maybe she was never happy being a wife and mother. She had abandoned him, his brother, and his dad and never looked back. Part of Coop wished he would never see her again, and the other part of him felt guilty for wishing such a thing.

With each footfall, the tension eased, and Coop's shoulders relaxed. The brisk morning air and Gus, being his usual goofy self, lightened his spirits.

Now, all he had to do was tell a dying man that his wife of twenty-five years conspired to kill his son and had just hired a hitman to kill him. There were still a few unanswered questions, and Coop wanted to get to the root of Adele's motives for her actions twenty-five years ago.

Coop welcomed the warm air that greeted him when he opened the back door of the office. Gus took to sprawling out across the cool tiles of the back entry while Coop poured himself some coffee and made his way to his office.

He didn't even get to finish his cup before the Covingtons arrived. AB ushered them in with a look of concern flashing in her eyes. Coop offered them seats and watched as Dax helped

Lindsay sit down. Her hair wasn't fixed, and her face was pale and drawn.

Frank looked even worse. All the joy of last night had evaporated, and the gray pallor of his skin worried Coop. AB brought in a tray of hot drinks and a pitcher of water before closing the door to Coop's office.

Dax cleared his throat and met Coop's eyes. "It's been a tough night and morning. Last night, we were going through photo albums, and Lindsay saw a picture of Adele from years ago at a company party. It threw her for a loop. She became distraught and so upset, we couldn't talk to her. She wanted to leave and go home, but then I had to tell her and Dad about Adele's call you overheard."

Coop's brow creased. "What was in the photo that caused you so much distress?"

Lindsay's wide eyes filled with tears. "Adele's scarf. The peacock. I didn't remember until I saw that picture last night, but she was at our house the day my mom died."

She reached for Dax's hand, and he recounted the rest of her story. "Lindsay was in her room upstairs in the afternoon, after school. She heard the front door slam and looked out the window. When she did, she saw a woman walking from the house, and the wind caught her scarf and sent it billowing to the side of her, making her reach out to grab it."

Dax explained Adele had never come to the house to see their mother in the past and had only been there a handful of times to drop things off for Frank or to attend a company picnic that Laura Beth hosted each summer. Dax continued, "Lindsay was only ten years old and after Mom died, she had a hard time, like all of us. She said she didn't remember that until she saw a photo in the album, and Adele was wearing that scarf. It had a bright blue and green peacock on it."

Dax squeezed Lindsay's hand and nodded to her. She spoke in a soft, almost whisper of a voice. "After I saw her leaving,

Mom ran into her bedroom, and I heard her crying, but when I knocked on her door, she just told me she needed to rest and to go play."

Frank's head and shoulders shook as he stifled a sob. "I don't understand why Adele would be at the house and what she said to upset my Laura Beth. She never mentioned being there."

Coop took a deep breath as his contempt for Adele increased. He reached for his coffee and took a sip to ease the sudden dryness in his throat. With Lindsay and Frank looking so vulnerable, he loathed the idea of adding to their pain. Today would get much worse.

Coop cleared his throat. "Originally, I wanted to meet with you to bring you up to date on the case, but after last night, things have gotten more complicated."

Frank nodded. "Dax told us that the police identified the remains, and that you overheard Adele on the phone." He shook his head, his fingers trembling as he reached for his cup. "I don't know what to make of it all. It's unbelievable."

"Does the name Jerry Corman mean anything to any of you?"

They all shook their heads. Dax said, "No, who is he?"

"The man Adele called last night. He's a retired probation officer who worked with Adele's first husband. He and Adele have known each other since then."

Dax's forehead wrinkled. "And she called him to have Dad killed?"

Coop glanced at Frank, hunched in his chair, seeming much smaller than he had been last night. "I'm afraid so. The police are involved and will be questioning him today. Probably as we speak. They've already brought in a man who confessed to the fire at the carnival site. He was a young man on probation, and Mr. Corman told him to go the site in Georgia and kill Dax. He wanted it to look like an accident and told him how to rig the pilot light to fill the RV with propane. Apparently, Corman controlled this man and other parolees with threats of harsher treatment and returns to prison or more lenient treatment in exchange for favors."

"Why would Adele want to kill Dax?" Frank's voice wobbled as he asked the question.

"I have a theory, but we'll need to wait to get that answer from Adele."

Lindsay sank lower in her chair and closer to her brother, who was seated between her and Frank. "How could we all have been tricked by her? She was so nice to me when I was growing up. I never want to see her again."

Dax put an arm around her. "We hardly got any sleep last night. Lindsay and I stayed over at Dad's to keep an eye on things. We told Adele we were visiting the cemetery this morning, so we could get away from the house without too many questions."

Coop took in the three of them. He wasn't sure how much more Frank and Lindsay could take without collapsing. "How about we find you a place to spend the day, where you'll be safe, and nobody will know where you are? You can get some rest, and I'll update you as soon as I know anything more. I'm afraid it could be a very long day."

Lindsay bobbed her head, tears splattering her cheeks. Dax reached for his dad's hand. "How about it, Dad? I think we could use some quiet and rest."

Frank's watery eyes met Coop's. "What did you have in mind?"

After Coop shared his idea, they agreed, and he asked AB to call Aunt Camille and explain the situation. After a few minutes, AB came into Coop's office and let them know Camille was on her way and would be happy to have them as guests for as long as necessary. AB offered to park Frank's car in her garage where it would be out of sight.

Coop took another sip of coffee. "We've got plenty of space, and my dad is there visiting right now. Aunt Camille will take good care of you and probably be cooking up a storm to feed you. Gus here…" He glanced at the dog lounging on the leather chair. "He's an excellent listener and will keep you company. I'll call Dax when I know more about what the police have learned."

Coop helped Frank from his chair, while Dax supported his sister. Frank hung onto Coop's hand with a strong grip. "This is above and beyond, Mr. Harrington. Please know how much I appreciate your help. If I weren't ill, I'd like to think I'd be stronger, but this is a real blow. It's making me question everything."

Coop walked them to the back door and moments later, Camille's sedan pulled into the parking lot. "I don't blame you for feeling overwhelmed. I also know it's probably impossible for you to relax but have something to eat and get some sleep. I'll know more later this afternoon or evening."

Between Coop and AB, they got the three of them and Gus into Camille's car, and she was already asking them their favorite foods and planning supper when she drove away. AB stood watching the car disappear around the corner. "I want nothing more than to nail that cold-blooded woman to the wall."

Coop took a few steps toward the door. "Me, too, AB. Me, too."

23

Coop and AB put away the donuts and washed all the mugs. They still hadn't heard from Ben and couldn't stand waiting any longer. AB drove Frank's car to her house and slipped it in the garage before joining Coop in his Jeep. Since it was approaching lunchtime, they stopped at the Pickle Barrel on the way and picked up a selection of sandwiches and salads to share with the detectives working on the weekend.

The precinct was quieter on a Saturday with most of the offices and cubicles empty, except for Ben, Kate, and Jimmy, who they found gathered around a conference table, watching the screens mounted on the wall that gave them a view of the interview rooms. Coop set the takeout bags on the table. "Thought you guys could use lunch."

While the five of them loaded their plates, Coop glanced at the screens, which showed two men in different rooms. "I take it Butch and the wire worked?"

Ben nodded. "Yeah, not as smooth as I was hoping, but eventually, we got there. We set up at a hole-in-the-wall diner near Butch's apartment. Butch got Corman to give him more details about the job. He was getting frustrated with Butch at one point and almost walked out, but thankfully, he stuck it out and then gave him point-by-point instructions on a carjacking scheme. He gave him directions to the Covington house, described Frank's car, and told him he'd try to arrange with the wife to have Frank run an errand on Sunday. Corman also made it clear not to leave any witnesses, so if Butch couldn't get to Frank alone, he was to take out Lindsay and Dax if they were with him."

AB's brows arched. "What a prince, huh?"

"Once Butch got Corman to name Frank and give the details, he hotfooted it to the bathroom and out the back door. We tried to convince him to go back in, but he was having none of it. We brought him back here and then watched Corman."

Kate reached for another napkin and added, "Instead of grabbing him right there, we waited. With Butch's statement, I was able to get a warrant to monitor Corman's phone and Adele's phone. I was hoping to get one more piece of evidence to link him to Adele and didn't have to wait long. Once Corman got back to his car, he made a call to her and asked her about arranging for Frank to be on his own on Sunday morning."

Coop nodded. "Smart, that will give you some leverage."

Jimmy gestured to the screen with the older man's image in it. "We picked him up right after that and read him his rights. He waived them and said he didn't need an attorney."

Ben grinned. "He thinks he's smart enough to outwit us. He's been in the system and knows how it works. He's also been running a criminal enterprise without so much as a whiff of suspicion for at least twenty-five years. I think he's pretty confident."

Kate polished off her sandwich and picked up a new bottle of water. "Let's go see what Mr. Corman has to tell us, Jimmy."

Coop and AB watched, along with Ben, as Kate and Jimmy entered the interview room. Kate announced their arrival and the time for the benefit of the recording and gave Corman the bottle of water. "Now, Mr. Corman, as we told you earlier, we received some rather alarming information from one of your prior probation clients, a Levi or Butch Jennings. He's alleging you approached him about murdering Frank Covington."

Corman sat back in his chair and smiled. "You know ex-cons, right? Always trying to pin their crimes on somebody else. Who better than their old parole officer, right?"

Jimmy opened a file folder. "So, you're denying the allegation that you approached Mr. Jennings for the purpose of arranging the killing of Frank Covington?"

Corman chuckled. "That's right, I'm denying it. Who's the court going to believe, me or some career criminal?"

Kate flipped a page in her file. "Mr. Jennings also stated that you employed him to carry out the murder of Dax Covington twenty-five years ago at a carnival site in rural Georgia. Do you have any knowledge of that allegation?"

His eyebrows arched, and he shook his head. "What have you got on this guy? He's obviously desperate and spinning tales about me to get off the hook for something."

Kate stared at him. "How about you answer the question, Mr. Corman. If you're innocent, the sooner we can get to the bottom of it, the sooner you can get out of here."

"Right, right. All business. Sure thing. I don't know anything about a fire at a carnival in Georgia twenty-five years ago."

Jimmy made a note. "So, you're also denying this allegation of arranging the attempted murder of Dax Covington and murder of Jacob Nathan Harris at the Royal Amusement carnival site in Walker County, Georgia in August of 1995?"

Corman nodded. "That's right, I am denying that allegation."

Kate's eyes narrowed. "We mentioned Frank and Dax Covington. Do you know either of these men?"

He shook his head. "No, ma'am."

She glanced at her notes. "How about Adele Covington?"

His forehead creased. "I don't recognize the name, sorry."

Jimmy tapped his pen on his notepad. "Ah, I think I know the problem. Maybe you knew her as Adele Pierce? Does that ring a bell?"

Corman's eyes widened. "Oh, yeah, Adele. She was married to a colleague. Poor guy died decades ago. I haven't kept in touch with Adele."

Kate nodded. "Is that a fact? You haven't had any contact with the woman you knew as Adele Pierce, now Adele Covington? When was the last time you saw or spoke to her?"

Corman blinked several times. "Wow, that was a long time ago. She and her son stayed in Murfreesboro for several years, and I think that's the last time I saw her. Had to be like thirty years ago, I guess."

Kate pulled out some papers from her folder. "So, how do you explain recent phone calls between you and Adele Covington?"

Corman squinted at the paper Kate pointed out with yellow highlights across two lines of numbers. He put his reading glasses on and studied the paper. His smile faded.

Kate pressed a button on a remote. "You might also be interested in a couple of conversations you had this morning." She played the recording of him talking with Butch in the diner and then the recording of the call he made to Adele.

He remained silent, glaring across the table at the two detectives.

"Funny thing, Mr. Corman. We never mentioned fire when we asked you about the murder in Georgia. I'm sure by now you understand what we have," said Kate. "Plenty enough to charge you with conspiracy to murder and murder of the young man in Georgia who was just recently identified. We'll be digging into every crevice of your life, and I have a feeling we'll find more ex-cons than Butch were doing you favors. The only glimmer of hope you have is in telling us everything you know about Adele and how you became the man she called to do her bidding. We'll put in a good word for you, and maybe you can live out the rest of your life in one of the better federal prisons, since your conspiracy activities across state lines will guarantee a federal charge."

Corman drummed his fingers atop the table and after several minutes, he sighed. "I think I'll take that lawyer now."

Kate and Jimmy gathered their papers and closed the files. "I have a feeling Adele is going to lay all of this at your feet, so now is the time to talk, but if you want to go the lawyer route, that's your choice."

The detectives stood and walked toward the door, but Corman remained silent.

Kate and Jimmy returned to the conference room and slammed their folders on the table. Kate paced the edge of the room. "Sorry, Boss. I thought for sure he'd spill his guts."

Ben stared at the screen on the wall. "Let's give him a little time alone and see what happens. We can bring Adele in with what we have. It would just make it easier if he would implicate her."

Coop caught his old friend's eye. "He's worried and not sure what to do. He thought he could talk his way out of it and without the recordings, he might have been able to do just that." He tilted his head toward the screen. "It's hard to get an attorney on the weekend. It can take hours." Coop winked and stood, clasping Ben on the shoulder.

Coop and AB followed Ben back to his office, while he left Kate and Jimmy to watch over Butch and Corman via the video screens.

Once the door to Ben's office closed, Coop told him they were keeping Frank and his kids safe at Aunt Camille's. He also told him about Lindsay's recollection of the day Adele came to visit at the house, prompted by the three of them going through old photo albums.

Ben's eyes narrowed. "Does she think she harmed her mother and maybe it wasn't a suicide?"

Coop shook his head. "I don't think so. Frank said there was no reason for Adele to be at the house that day, and Lindsay just knows that after Adele left, her mother was crying and inconsolable. Laura Beth told her she wanted to lie down and to play in her room."

Ben tapped some keys on his keyboard and stared at the screen. "The report on her death shows Frank was the one who found her when he got home from work. He arrived just before seven o'clock and was surprised Laura Beth wasn't downstairs and dinner hadn't been started. He called 911 at six fifty-nine and said he found empty pill bottles and vodka in her room. No suicide note was ever found."

Coop nodded. "Frank said Laura Beth had been prescribed some sleeping pills and anti-anxiety medication. She had been struggling since the carnival accidents. She didn't drink, so he was surprised at the vodka."

"No foul play was suspected. The medical examiner ruled it a suicide."

"I don't doubt it was a suicide, but I know her visit that day is causing both Lindsay and Frank great distress. I'd like to get to the bottom of it, so they get some answers."

"Do you have any ideas on how to do that?" asked Ben.

"As a matter of fact, I do." Coop took a seat in front of Ben's desk.

24

Saturday evening, Frank was resting against pillows in the hospital bed of his private room at Vanderbilt University Medical Center. When Adele came through the door, his eyes were closed, and the room was quiet and lit only by a soft lamp in the corner.

She looked at the empty chair next to his bed and shook her head. "Where's Lindsay?"

She put her purse down and slipped into the chair, staring at her husband. "How are you, darling?" she whispered.

His eyes fluttered. "Tired, Adele, very tired."

"When Dax picked me up, he said Lindsay was with you. She shouldn't have left you alone."

"She just went to get me some ice chips."

Adele huffed. "You'd think with all the support and donations we've given this place over the years, your daughter wouldn't have to fetch you ice. These nurses need to be more attentive." She patted his hand. "I'm here now, sweetheart, don't worry. Dax said they expect to keep you for several days."

She sat back in her chair and watched the bag of fluid drip

into the intravenous line in Frank's hand. "Dax said you practically collapsed at the cemetery. I told you, you've been doing too much. The party was too much."

Frank's eyes opened and focused on her. "Why did you come to the house the day Laura Beth died?"

Adele's eyes went wide. "What are you talking about, dear? I'm afraid whatever they've got you on has made you delirious."

"Lindsay remembered you being there after she saw a photo in the album last night. The one with you wearing that bright peacock scarf. She saw you at the house that day and remembered the scarf. You were there, Adele. I want to know why."

She brushed a spec of lint from her jacket. "I'm not sure why this is on your mind, Frank."

He sighed. "I don't have much time left, Adele. I think you owe me an explanation. Why were you visiting Laura Beth that afternoon?"

She stood and reached for the pillows behind his head, smoothing the pillowcases. "I knew she was having a hard time, dealing with the accidents, and I knew it was weighing on you and the children."

"How was she when you left her that afternoon?"

"Better, I thought. Obviously..." Her voice trailed off without finishing her thoughts.

"She wasn't crying uncontrollably when you left her that afternoon? Think long and hard, Adele. Lindsay has remembered that day quite clearly now."

Her eyes narrowed and her jaw hardened as she looked at her husband. With venom in her voice she said, "I went there to tell her she was weak. Far too weak for you. You and the children needed a strong wife and mother. A wife who would support you and not fold and wither under pressure."

Tears leaked from Frank's eyes as he looked up at Adele. "Why would you do that? She was in a fragile state."

Adele shrugged. "I told her she needed to snap out of it or quit dragging out the inevitable. I told her she could make it all go away, and it would be easy. Just like going to sleep." Adele's lips curled into a sinister smile.

"You… you gave her the vodka, didn't you?"

She brushed a hand over his forehead. "Yes, my dear. But I did it for you and Dax and Lindsay. Laura Beth was never going to be able to function. She would have just drained all of you the longer it went on." She sighed and sat back down. "I was there and knew I could pick up the pieces and take proper care of you and Lindsay. Dax was grown, but Lindsay was just a child and needed a mother who would cherish her. Indulge her."

Frank swallowed hard. "You had no right, Adele. That was my family."

She patted his hand again. "No need to work yourself up about it, dear. It's ancient history. Everything's going to be just fine."

Frank's shoulders shook as he listened to her detached voice.

"I'll make sure and call Mr. Harrington and tell him you're in the hospital and won't be able to keep your Monday appointment. I'm sure he'll understand."

The lock clicked on an interior door on the wall opposite the bed, and Coop and AB stepped into the room. Coop looked into Adele's cold eyes. "No need to do that, Mrs. Covington. Frank already met with me and made the changes to his will and estate. Everything is set."

She stood and looked from her husband to Coop, darting her eyes between the two with her mouth hanging open. "What do you mean?"

"Frank was waiting to tell you about the changes and what it means for you and your son. He didn't want to spoil Lindsay's birthday and was going to tell you this weekend, but then these pesky questions came up about the day of Laura Beth's death."

She whipped her head back to Frank. "What have you done?" She spat out the words like an enraged crone. Gone was the illusion of youthful beauty and any pretense of caring about the man who had been her husband for twenty-five years.

Coop took a few steps toward her. "He just made sure his business and fortune will stay with his family. His children. Dax and Lindsay. He had also made provisions for you and Gavin, but that may be complicated now. We've had to make a few adjustments to it just today."

She focused her anger on Coop. "What complications?" Spittle flew from her mouth as she raised her voice.

Kate and Jimmy came through the door of the hospital room and approached Adele. Kate towered over the woman and said, "Adele Covington, you are under the arrest for conspiracy to commit murder and the murder of Jacob Nathan Harris and conspiracy to commit the murder of Frank Covington." Jimmy put the handcuffs on her and read her the rights she was guaranteed by law.

Coop glanced at the metal cuffs on her wrists. "Those complications." He started to walk away and then turned back to Adele. "Oh, Frank was also wearing a recording device, and we were watching everything from the room next door. I think the entire video of your conversation with your dying husband will make a strong impression on the jury."

Adele's eyes went cold, and she looked at her husband and then at Coop and AB. "This is preposterous. My lawyer will have me out in no time and the lot of you up on harassment charges."

As Jimmy ushered her out of the room, Coop said, "You'll probably need a public defender, Adele. Mr. Jennings and his firm are Frank's lawyers, and you no longer have access to his bank accounts or any other Covington assets."

After Kate and Jimmy left with Adele, Dax and Lindsay came through the door and ran to their father's bedside. They both hugged him, and he patted Lindsay on the back of her head, murmuring to her and assuring her that everything would be all right.

Dax rang for the nurse and moments later, she came through the door and removed the saline line from Frank's hand. Lindsay and AB stepped into the hallway, while Dax and Coop stayed with Frank to help him gather his things and get dressed.

Frank hadn't been happy to wear a hospital gown, but Coop had persuaded him that Adele had to be convinced he was ill. Looking at his sallow color, it didn't take much of a stretch of the imagination.

Frank's doctor, who said Frank was a bit dehydrated and could use some saline, was happy to accommodate his request for the use of the private room for a few hours. While Frank was there, the doctor checked him out and while he didn't ask questions, he reminded Frank that stress wasn't good for his condition and wanted him to get some rest.

When Frank emerged, dressed, but looking less frail than he had in the hospital bed, Dax and Lindsay each looped an arm in his. "Let's go home, Dad," said Dax.

"You all get some rest, and we'll be in touch tomorrow and update you," Coop said.

Frank turned, before walking toward the exit. "Thank you again and thank Camille for me. It was a lovely respite to spend the day with her and your dad."

Coop nodded and glanced at AB. He slung an arm around her shoulder and said, "Let's go grab supper before we head down to the precinct. Aunt Camille will have it waiting on us."

"Not to mention she'll be dying for an update on the case." AB laughed as they traversed the hallways to get to the parking area.

"You know, I thought Marlene was the worst mom in the universe, but I think Adele takes that prize."

She bumped her shoulder into his. "Marlene's a runner-up in

that contest, I guess. It's hard to beat someone as cold hearted as Adele."

25

After a quick supper and lots of questions, Camille sent them back to the precinct laden down with containers of food for the detective squad. Gus went with them on this trip and after getting lots of belly rubs from the officers and detectives, he hurried into Ben's office where he flopped on the dog bed Ben kept in the corner.

Ben and Jimmy and Kate dug into the chicken alfredo casserole Aunt Camille had sent, along with the salad, fresh rolls, and cookies she included in the basket. Coop let them eat while he and AB read through the working file Ben slid across the table.

As Coop and Ben had predicted, Corman caved after a couple of hours and said he wanted to make a statement rather than wait for his lawyer. He outlined his relationship with Adele, which was built on an infatuation with her that started years ago when he worked with her husband. He was willing to do anything to help her after Roger died. He confirmed what the neighbor had told Coop about him mowing the lawn and taking care of things around the house. He had hoped for a romantic relationship with her and was trying to win her over.

He had lost hope and lost touch with her when she married

Frank and moved away from Murfreesboro. He admitted when Adele reached out to him for help twenty-five years ago, he was so anxious to hear from her, he was willing to do anything. Corman had indeed run a criminal enterprise, blackmailing those on probation to commit mostly small-time offenses while Corman pocketed money for coordinating the operation.

He had accumulated a substantial amount of money over the years. The search warrant they executed at his home netted tens of thousands in cash, along with lots of gold and silver coins. Corman provided a list of dozens of ex-cons he had used over the last decades.

Adele had paid him five hundred dollars for his role in arranging the fire and death of Dax. Back then, she was a mess and wanted to keep her son out of trouble. She told Corman that Gavin had been the one pressuring the carnival bosses to save money on maintenance. He was young and trying to prove himself and had made mistakes. Like Mrs. Davis had told Coop, she would do anything for her precious boy. Even kill for him.

This time, when Adele called him, Corman wasn't so eager to please her and demanded much more money to arrange the murder of Frank. He also told her if he weren't alone, the price would double or triple. She promised him whatever he wanted, and he held out a glimmer of hope that they would get together when it was over.

Coop shook his head, and AB pushed the folder away from her. She made a gagging sound and said, "I feel like I need a shower after reading it. I can't imagine sitting in the same room with this creep."

Kate rolled her eyes. "He's a charmer, but at least he gave us everything we need on Adele."

Jimmy finished the last bite from his plate. "Adele is the most callous and cold-hearted woman I remember interviewing."

Kate nodded. "Yep, it does my heart good that we arrested her on a weekend. No judge until Monday, so she'll get to spend some time behind bars. She's the epitome of a soulless narcissist."

Ben took a cookie from the plastic container. "She was confident and arrogant until we played her the video of Corman telling us the whole story. That knocked the wind out of her sails. She was begging for a deal in the end, but the district attorney told her she had no bargaining power. He told her his office is contemplating the death penalty."

AB's eyes widened. "I bet that shut the old bat up."

Ben nodded. "We brought Gavin in to interview and after we told him his mother had been arrested for murder and conspiracy to murder, his attitude also changed. He confessed to the scheme to save money at the carnival that led to the accidents. He said Adele told him not to worry and that she'd handle everything and cover for him."

Kate reached across the table for the cookies. "Thing is, I do believe he didn't know his mother had arranged to have Dax killed. He was genuinely shocked and sickened by it. When we told him about her plot to have Frank killed, he broke down."

Coop's brow creased. "Lindsay and Dax said Adele was smothering. I wonder if deep down, Gavin thought the same about her. They seemed devoted to one another, but to have your mother kill for you to cover up your idiotic business methods would take that loyalty to a new level."

Ben bobbed his head. "Yeah, I think he found it revolting and is probably going to need some type of counseling. He kept muttering that his mother told him none of the accidents were his fault. She blamed it all on the carnival bosses and the pressure Huck put on Gavin at work. He never even asked to see her or inquired about bail or anything else. He just left here in a daze."

Coop shook his head. "What a nightmare. I'm just glad we were able to get Frank's will and his estate amended again. Frank still has a soft spot for Gavin, even after we told him our investigation led us to believe Gavin was the one who had given the directive about forgoing maintenance and cutting back on expenses. He may not have intentionally caused the accidents, but he bears the responsibility. Frank blames himself for not keeping a better eye on him. He elected to keep him in his will, but Adele gets nothing, except the assets she had when she came into the marriage, as outlined in their prenuptial agreement. Frank had agreed to give Adele a substantial amount of money and property, but when he learned the truth, Dax and Lindsay convinced him to change that provision."

Coop sighed. "I also drafted divorce proceedings. We're going to meet with him tomorrow to go over them and everything else. I promised to call Dax tonight, but Frank needs some peace and rest right now."

Ben leaned back in his chair. "Poor guy. Having to deal with all of this on top of his health issue can't be easy."

Aunt Camille insisted she make Sunday supper for the Covington family. Coop tried to dissuade her, but she wouldn't hear of it. She called Lindsay and within twenty minutes, it was a done deal.

Coop invited AB, and she came over early to help Coop clean and straighten his home office. They welcomed Frank with his two children at his side and after updating them on the case the police had against Adele and the likelihood that she would remain in jail until her trial, Coop reviewed the divorce documents. Harrington and Associates didn't normally handle divorces, but Coop made an exception in Frank's case.

Dax cleared his throat. "We understand Dad wanting to make sure Gavin gets something in the will, but Lindsay and I don't want him around the company. I arranged to have the locks changed this morning, and we boxed up his personal possessions and had them messengered to his home. It's going to take me more time, maybe a long time, to forgive him. He started all of this. We lost our mother because of him, and I'm not open to having him around at all."

Dax glanced at his dad. "With time, I hope I can forgive him, like Dad has, but right now, it's too fresh. Too painful. When it comes to Adele, I'm not sure any of us will ever find it in our hearts to forgive her. She's nothing but a vile human being with the cold heart of a killer."

Lindsay didn't say anything but bobbed her head as Dax spoke.

Coop nodded. "I don't blame you. I think what she's done is unforgiveable, but I'm confident justice will prevail. I suspect her case won't go to trial. The evidence is overwhelming and with the confessions from Butch and Corman, she has no defense. I'm sure her lawyer will do his best to negotiate a sentence for her, but imagine she'll be spending the rest of her life in prison."

AB caught Frank's eye. "What's important for you, is to focus on your health and putting this behind you. We'll take care of all the legal matters and do our best to keep the time you have to appear in court to an absolute minimum. We want you and Dax and Lindsay to live your life and make up for some lost time."

Frank smiled, and Dax reached for his dad's hand. "Our sole focus is getting Dad healthy. We're going to that new doctor tomorrow, and Ed, dad's friend you met at the party, he and his son, who just moved back to Nashville, they're going to take care of running the insurance office for us until we're back on our feet."

"That's great news," said Coop. "Lifelong friends are hard to come by and are more valuable than anything." He glanced across the desk at AB. "AB and I are lifelong friends and would do anything for each other. I'd be lost without her, so I'm glad you have Ed, and he's willing to help."

Frank smiled and winked at AB. "I'd say you two are quite lucky to have each other."

Aunt Camille's voice hollered out that supper was ready. Frank signed the divorce papers where AB had attached the sticky flags and slid them back to Coop. He waved at his children. "You two go on ahead. I just need a word with Mr. Harrington."

AB followed them out of Coop's office, clicking the door shut behind her.

Frank pulled an envelope from his jacket pocket. "I can never repay you for all you've done for me… for my family." Tears glistened in his eyes. "I'm still in shock about everything that Adele did. I'm replaying the last twenty-five years in my mind and kicking myself for not seeing what had to be right in front of me. Dax says he isn't sure he'll ever forgive Gavin or Adele. I'm not sure I'll ever forgive myself."

He waved his hand in front of him. "All that aside, I owe you more than a check. You've given me my son back and a chance to live the rest of my days in peace. I truly owe you my life. I've added in a bit of a bonus to your fee to show my gratitude and appreciation." He handed Coop the envelope.

"Oh, one more thing." Frank reached into his pocket and pulled out a keychain. "Here's a key to the condo in Florida. We only use it a few weeks a year and at the moment, I don't have any plans to use it for the foreseeable future. My secretary will email you all the particulars you need and whenever you or AB or your family want to use it, it's yours. The calendar is available online, so we'll never double book. I'm hoping Dax and Lindsay get some use out of it, but like they said, right now we're focused on this new treatment plan."

Coop stared at the key, speechless. "I don't know what to say. Are you sure about this? It's so generous and not necessary."

Frank grinned and chuckled. "I'm sure. I want people who enjoy it to use it."

Coop smiled and tucked the key into his desk drawer. "This will make AB the happiest woman on the planet. She loved it there and didn't want to leave. Maybe I'll give her a few days off and a ticket to Tampa as a reward for all the work she's done on your case."

Frank clasped a hand on Coop's shoulder. "That, my boy, is the smartest thing you've said all evening." He walked toward the door with Coop. "You know, Mr. Harrington, some of the most successful marriages are between best friends. That's how Laura Beth and I started out."

Coop chuckled as he led Frank down the hallway. "AB and I are best friends, and we work so well together. I don't think I'd ever want to mess that up."

"Never say never, Mr. Harrington."

26

TWO MONTHS LATER

Coop and AB took charge of the luggage and let Charlie and Aunt Camille gawk out the windows at the Tampa skyline. It had taken several days to convince Charlie that the ninety-minute flight from Nashville would be painless and worth it once he saw the coastline. Leaving Gus was harder than Coop anticipated, but Ben promised to take good care of him and reminded Coop they would only be gone a few days.

As with their first trip to Clearwater Beach, AB had arranged the shuttle service, and they were soon whisked away from the airport and across the bay. Aunt Camille never stopped chattering the entire way, asking the driver the name of every landmark they came across.

He dropped them at the resort, and Coop thanked him for his patience with a hefty tip. AB led the way to the lobby, and they checked in at the front desk and rode the elevator to the seventh floor. She slipped the key into the door and held it open for Charlie and Aunt Camille, who both gasped at the stunning view of the ocean and beach below.

Charlie took off his baseball cap and waved it in front of his face. "It's beautiful here, but I'm not sure I can take the humidity. I'd never manage it in the summer if this is how it is in early April."

"You'll adjust after a few days, Dad. AB will have you down at the beach under an umbrella or dipping your toes in the pool and sipping a cold drink, and you'll forget all about it."

Aunt Camille was out on the balcony, soaking in the view and watching the waves arrive on the white sandy beach. Coop carried her luggage into the room she and AB would share and toted his bag and his dad's to the other bedroom.

Coop added swim trunks to his favorite soft gray t-shirt, lettered with BEFORE COFFEE: JUDGMENTAL & SARCASTIC AFTER COFFEE: JUDGMENTAL & SARCASTIC, BUT FASTER. In no time, the others changed into beachwear and headed downstairs to have lunch at the restaurant near the pool. After a quick meal, AB led them to the gorgeous pool. Aunt Camille wasn't much for swimming but wore a loose muumuu in a tropical print and looked quite content tucked under a huge sun umbrella with her nose in a book she was trying to finish for her book club.

The staff kept them stocked with lemonade and iced teas, and Charlie, who wasn't a big fan of pools, enjoyed himself remarking how good the water and movement felt on his knee. After several hours swimming and lounging, they dried off and went for a walk down to the beach, where they all dipped their toes into the ocean.

Living in Nevada, Charlie didn't get to the ocean much, but his grin told Coop he was happy. Coop relished the gentle waves rolling in and over his feet and ankles and found the feel of it and the expanse of the water in front of him mesmerizing. Charlie stood next to him and stared at the ocean. "I see why you pestered me to come. It's quite a remarkable view here. I've never seen such white sand."

Coop chuckled. "I know. I didn't want you to miss out. If you come back and visit us again, we'll plan another trip. It's great during the winter months."

Charlie grinned. "I might take you up on that. It's been wonderful being here with you and Camille. And AB and Gus, of course. I'm so proud of you, Coop. You're a good man and notwithstanding the occasional drama from your mother, you have a happy and full life here. I should have made an effort to visit more often."

Coop turned to face his dad. "You know, we'd love it if you came more often and stayed longer. I'm serious about the idea of spending half the year with us. I know you'd miss Jack and the grandkids, but you could spend late spring and summer back home, and then maybe head out here for late fall and winter. Aunt Camille would be over the moon, and so would I."

Charlie smiled and put an arm around his son's shoulder. "I like the sound of that. I need to get my head around it and figure out how to make it happen. Seeing Frank's regret at missing all those years with Dax puts life in perspective, doesn't it?"

Coop squeezed his dad's shoulders. "It sure does, Dad." They walked down the beach several yards while AB and Camille took photos.

"Speaking of Frank," said Charlie, "we should probably be heading back upstairs to get cleaned up for the big event."

Coop turned around, and they made their way down the beach and back to AB and Aunt Camille. With two bathrooms in the condo, it didn't take long for them to get showered and dressed.

Aunt Camille and AB wore dresses they had purchased for the occasion, and the boutique owner back in Nashville assured them they were perfect for Florida, casual and cosmopolitan. Whatever that meant.

The best Charlie and Coop could muster were light beige khaki pants and tropical shirts. Coop thought they looked like Hawaiian tourists, but AB told them it was perfect for the weather and the resort atmosphere.

With zero fashion sense, Coop put his complete faith in AB and led the way down the hall to the Covingtons' condo. Dax opened the door and welcomed them with a huge smile. "Oh, I'm so glad you're all here. I hope the condo we got for you is comfortable."

AB nodded. "It's lovely. Thank you for doing that for us."

"Come in and meet everyone and get settled. Lindsay took Dad out to the beach for a few minutes, but they'll be here shortly."

He led them through the hallway to the open area Coop remembered from his last visit. A huge buffet was set up in the dining area, and several people were gathered in the living room and on the balcony, sipping drinks. AB poked Coop with her elbow and pointed at three men talking, all of whom wore tropical print shirts and khaki pants. "What did I tell you?"

They had just gotten their drinks when Dax announced Lindsay and his dad were on their way up from the lobby. He ushered everyone into corners to try to hide as many people as possible, and they waited in silence.

A few minutes later, the door clicked open, and Frank came around the corner, and the guests erupted with shouts of "Surprise!" Frank's eyes went wide, and he took a couple of steps back and then grinned.

"Ah, you two." He searched out Dax and reached for Lindsay's hand behind him. "You got me. I thought we agreed to a quiet birthday celebration."

Dax hugged his dad and then looked out over the guests who had all made the trip to Florida to surprise Frank. "This isn't just a birthday celebration, it's so much more. Lindsay and I wanted to do something special this year. Dad had some tests and a visit with his doctor last week, and we got the best news we could have hoped for."

Tears filled Dax's eyes as he looked at his dad. "The treatments are working. Dad's bloodwork is great and while the doctor said he doesn't like to use the word cure, he told us he's optimistic, and he expects Dad to get stronger and healthier over the next few months."

The guests cheered and applauded at the wonderful news.

Dax handed Frank a glass of lemonade, and he took a long sip before surveying the room. "I'm so very lucky to have these two wonderful children and all of you in my life. These past few months have been a rollercoaster ride of emotions. With Dax home and the horrible tragedies from decades ago explained and put to rest, I'm thankful for all of you and your support. It's been difficult to say the least, but your love and friendship has made it easier. Thank you for being here today. It means more to me than you'll ever know."

His voice cracked as he finished his sentence, and fresh tears dotted his cheeks. A few other people raised their glasses and toasted Frank and his family, wishing him nothing but happiness in the years to come.

With the tributes over, Lindsay invited everyone to help themselves to the buffet and promised a special birthday cake for dessert. Coop mingled with the guests and nibbled on the barbecued pork sliders and nachos. After a bit of cajoling, AB finally convinced him to try the mini fish tacos, and he hated to admit it, but he liked them.

As he finished one of them, Frank came up to him. "I'm thrilled you all made the trip down here. Dax and Lindsay pulled off quite the coup. I had no idea they had all this planned."

"We're so happy you're feeling better and got such great news from the doctor. I'm sure having the case closed on Adele helps with the stress. I'm glad it's over, and there was no trial. None of you need to relive that trauma."

The pain flashed in Frank's eyes like a film he had to blink away. "It's for the best. I've already spent far too much time looking back. The guilt can be overwhelming, but with Dax and

Lindsay's help, I'm focused on the future. I need to close the book on the rest of it, or I'll go mad. I elected not to visit Adele in prison. I decided she had manipulated me for the last time. I did meet with Gavin. He sold his house and is moving to California. I don't envy him and his demons."

Frank took a sip from his tropical frozen drink. "The doctor's good report helped immensely. Now, I feel like I can make some plans, and it won't be an exercise in futility or just placating my kids."

Coop nodded and looked across the room at AB, Aunt Camille, and Charlie, all laughing. "That's the best part of life. Spending time with those you love."

The arrival of the birthday cake, a strawberry and cream layered one, decorated with sparkling glitter, cut their conversation short. Lindsay collected Frank and together, they found Dax, and the three of them stood, arms linked, behind the festive cake as everyone sang to Frank.

Coop watched as Frank cut the first slice and grinned like a little kid when he took a bite of it. AB stood next to Coop and bumped her shoulder against his arm. "Feels good, doesn't it?"

He turned toward her. "What's that?"

"To have played a part in all of them being together and happy. I had my doubts a few times during this case, but being here, watching the three of them now, makes my heart happy."

He put an arm around her. "You're right, AB. We did good." The four of them took their cake out to the balcony and watched the sun dip into the Gulf of Mexico. As it did, ribbons of gold and orange hung above the water.

Coop leaned closer to AB and whispered, "Maybe we should open a satellite office down here."

She winked and raised her glass. "What a great idea."

EPILOGUE

C *old Killer* is the fourth book in the Cooper Harrington Detective Novels. You'll discover a new case in each book in the series, but the characters you've come to know will continue throughout the series. Tammy plans to continue this series until she runs out of cases for Coop. The books don't have to be read in order but are more enjoyable when you do, since you'll learn more about Coop's backstory as the series unfolds. If you're a new reader to Coop's books, you won't want to miss the other novels in the series.

If you've missed reading any, here are the links to the entire series, in order.

Killer Music
Deadly Connection
Dead Wrong
Cold Killer
Deadly Deception

ACKNOWLEDGMENTS

It's been so long since I've spent time with Coop, AB, Gus, and Aunt Camille and writing this book felt like visiting old friends. I feel that way about the characters in my Hometown Harbor Series as well. I miss the characters when I have to be away from them and work on other projects.

My favorite part of writing fiction is character creation, and this book gave me some great opportunities. Coop's mother makes another appearance in *Cold Killer* and as usual, she's a handful. Coop's dad, Charlie, is still staying with him while he recuperates. Having Charlie in the cast of characters has been fun and enhances the story.

As always, I'm thankful for my early readers, who are diligent when it comes to reading my manuscripts. My dad is still my greatest source of expertise in all things crime, being in law enforcement for over thirty years. We had several conversations about the "what if" questions that always fuel these books. This one started based on one of his cold cases from decades ago.

I love the new covers I'm using from Elizabeth Mackey Graphic Design. She is beyond talented and never disappoints. Gus tells me he expects lots of extra cookies for all the posing that went into the photoshoot for the new covers. Many thanks to my editor, Susan, for helping me polish the story.

I'm grateful for the support and encouragement of my friends and family as I continue to pursue my dream of writing. I appreciate all of the readers who have taken the time to provide a review on Amazon, BookBub, or Goodreads. These reviews are especially important in promoting future books, so if you enjoy my novels, please consider leaving a review. I also encourage you to follow me on major book retailers, and you'll be the first to know about new releases.

Remember to visit my website at www.tammylgrace.com or follow me on Facebook at www.facebook.com/tammylgrace. books to keep in touch—I'd love to hear from you.

FROM THE AUTHOR

Thank you for reading the fourth book in the Cooper Harrington Detective Series. These mystery books are designed to be stand-alone reads, but I recommend reading them in order, as you'll learn more about the recurring characters. If you enjoyed it and are a fan of women's fiction, you'll want to try my HOMETOWN HARBOR SERIES and my GLASS BEACH COTTAGE SERIES.

The two books I've written as Casey Wilson, A DOG'S HOPE and A DOG'S CHANCE, both have received enthusiastic support from my readers and, if you're a dog lover, are must-reads.

If you enjoy holiday stories, be sure to check out my CHRISTMAS IN SILVER FALLS SERIES and HOMETOWN CHRISTMAS SERIES. They are small-town Christmas stories of hope, friendship, and family. I'm also one of the authors of the bestselling SOUL SISTERS AT CEDAR MOUNTAIN LODGE SERIES, centered around a woman who opens her heart and home to four foster girls one Christmas.

I'm also one of the founding authors of My Book Friends and invite you to join this fun group of readers and authors on

Facebook. I'd love to send you my exclusive interview with the canine companions in my Hometown Harbor Series as a thank-you for joining my exclusive group of readers. You can sign up by following this link: https://wp.me/P9umIy-e

I hope you'll connect with me on social media. You can find me on Facebook, where I have a page and a special group for my readers and follow me on Amazon and BookBub, so you'll know when I have a new release or a deal. Be sure to download the free novella, HOMETOWN HARBOR: THE BEGINNING. It's a prequel to FINDING HOME that I know you'll enjoy.

If you did enjoy this book or any of my other books, I'd be grateful if you took a few minutes to leave a short review on Amazon, BookBub, Goodreads, or any of the other retailers you use.

MORE FROM TAMMY L. GRACE

GLASS BEACH COTTAGE SERIES

Beach Haven

Moonlight Beach

Beach Dreams

WRITING AS CASEY WILSON

A Dog's Hope

A Dog's Chance

WISHING TREE SERIES

The Wishing Tree

Wish Again

Overdue Wishes

SISTERS OF THE HEART SERIES

Greetings from Lavender Valley

Pathway to Lavender Valley

Sanctuary at Lavender Valley

Blossoms at Lavender Valley

Comfort in Lavender Valley

Reunion in Lavender Valley

Remember to subscribe to Tammy's exclusive group of readers for your gift, only available to readers on her mailing list. **Sign up at www. tammylgrace.com. Follow this link to subscribe at https://wp.me/ P9umIy-e** and you'll receive the exclusive interview she did with all the canine characters in her Hometown Harbor Series.

Follow Tammy on Facebook by liking her page. You may also follow Tammy on book retailers or at BookBub by clicking on the follow button.

ABOUT THE AUTHOR

Tammy L. Grace is the *USA Today* bestselling and award-winning author of the Cooper Harrington Detective Novels, the best-selling Hometown Harbor Series, and the Glass Beach Cottage Series, along with several sweet Christmas novellas. Tammy also writes under the pen name of Casey Wilson for Bookouture and Grand Central Publishing. You'll find Tammy online at www.tammylgrace.com where you can join her mailing list and be part of her exclusive group of readers. Connect with Tammy on social media by clicking on the icons below and liking her author pages on major book retailers.

facebook.com/tammylgrace.books

twitter.com/TammyLGrace

instagram.com/authortammygrace

bookbub.com/authors/tammy-l-grace

goodreads.com/tammylgrace

pinterest.com/tammylgrace

Made in the USA
Monee, IL
10 April 2024

56746260R00142